Falling for the Sheikh

Ultimate Billionaires Book 2

Barbara McMahon

One

Her father was going to kill her, Sara Kinsale thought, barely suppressing a groan. She looked around the dusty cell and grimaced. She'd been here two days. Two days when she should have been at the hotel in Staboul. Two days stuck in some backwater jail in the very country in which her father was trying to nail the biggest deal of all time. When he needed everything perfect to convince the powers that be that his company would broker the most favorable deal for the newly up-for-grabs oil leases.

She jumped up from the narrow cot and began to pace the tiny cell. She'd alternated between contemplating her parents' reaction while trying to come up with a solution to her dilemma that might allow her to keep this from them—and the world press.

If her father didn't kill her, her mother would guilt her to death with her soft sighs and her telling looks. She'd ask her father a million times, "Where did we go wrong?"

Sara blew her bangs off her forehead and leaned against the hard cinder block wall. She knew the drill. Her parents hadn't gone wrong, that was on her. But not intentionally. Things always seemed to go sideways when she was involved.

First, she hadn't settled on a career—not like her sister the attorney. Or her brother the nuclear physicist. Or even her mother, the perfect hostess, charity coordinator and helpmate to an international businessman.

She'd tried to find a niche that she could call her own. Acting hadn't worked out, to the great relief of her parents. Nor nursing. She got queasy at the sight of blood. Being a childcare worker proved to be lots of fun—she loved playing with the kids. But her lack of discipline with the children got her fired from both jobs she'd found.

The latest job bordered on acceptable. Photojournalism was a respected profession. If she proved herself, maybe her family would begin to see her as a contributing member of society and not a flake who never settled on anything.

Only now she'd blown that as well.

The editor of the U.S. tabloid newspaper that hired her had been thrilled when she'd told him about her upcoming visit to Kamtansin. It was recently in the news as one of the newly emerging Arabian countries on the Mediterranean Sea. The plum assignment of getting photos of some of the royal family of the small Arabian country had been hers for the asking.

The assignment to interview some of the leading members of Kamtansin society seemed a piece of cake in Los Angeles. Especially since several members of the family were in deep negotiations with her father over the oil leases.

She'd meet them, bowl them over with her charm and get those interviews and pictures.

The reality proved one hundred percent opposite to what she'd expected. She'd been refused interviews and refused photo opportunities.

The worst, however, was being apprehended while trying to film the summer retreat of one of the leading families-despite being warned not to approach them. Now she languished in some horrible jail that didn't even have basic facilities.

Worse, she'd been accused of being a spy!

She hadn't been allowed to contact the U.S. embassy. Nor call her father. She hadn't been permitted to seek an attorney. She hadn't been able to do anything but worry herself sick about the predicament she was in. She'd never take American rights for granted again.

Her parents would be frantic. They had no idea where she was. While on the one hand that was a good thing considering where she actually was—on the other hand, if her father knew, he'd move heaven and earth to get her free.

She'd stayed one night in the hotel with them when she first arrived. Then she'd boldly plunged into her assignment to get something on film after the string of refusals through normal channels. Even though she wasn't able to get as close to the summer enclave as she wanted, the telephoto lens allowed her to capture the smallest details.

She'd scarcely shot two pictures before being captured.

Her parents' worry couldn't compare with her own.

The laws of this country were completely unknown to her. Would she be granted a trial or end up remaining in this hot, dusty cell forever—with no one in her family ever knowing what happened to her?

The door opened. At least there'd been more privacy than she expected. The door to the small cinder block cell was solid wood, with only a small square about midway that permitted food to pass through twice a day and allowed the jailors to check on her from time to time. Like she was going to escape? The only window in the room was equally small and set too high in the wall for her to even reach.

The tall man dressed in an army uniform motioned with his head. He was the one who gave her the food each day. He didn't speak English, and she didn't understand a word of Arabic.

Sara brushed down her khaki trousers and shook her shirt a little. After two days and two nights with no washing, the sharp creases and crisp look long since faded, she felt rumpled, dirty and tired. And more than a bit scared.

"I want to call the U.S. embassy," she said. She was sure the man didn't understand English, but she'd go down trying!

He remained silent, pointing down the hall.

She walked toward the door. Once within reach, he clasped her arm in a firm grip then marched her down the long corridor to the wide stairs at the end. Again she wondered what they thought she was going to do—flee from the building and face endless miles of burning desert sand and scorching heat with no vehicle to carry her back to safety? Her rental car was probably still hidden in the hill behind the summer villa. And she had no idea where that was in relation to where she was now. Once arrested, the drive to the prison took more than forty-five minutes. Without a map and some clear directions, she didn't even know in which direction the capital city lay.

They climbed two flights. He knocked on a door and upon hearing the reply from within, opened it, pushing Sara in before releasing her.

Sara quickly glanced around the austere office—minimal furnishings, no coverings on the windows.

A man stood by one of the tall windows, gazing out over the desert landscape. Slowly he turned to look at her.

Sara felt a warm tendril of awareness curl within when his eyes met hers. He easily topped six feet. His hair was black, gleaming in the sunshine beaming in through the tall window. His eyes were dark, fathomless, with an uncompromising glint in them as he studied her. His cheekbones were high with taut tanned skin covering them. Power seemed to radiate from him, enhanced by the exquisitely tailored suit, the wide shoulders, the decidedly masculine stance.

Suddenly aware of her own bedraggled appearance, she wished she'd been able to brush her hair or wash her face. Something!

Then the absurdity of the situation hit her. She wanted to get out of jail, not make some kind of good impression on a stranger. One, moreover, who apparently had some control over her incarceration, otherwise why was she here?

"I wish to call the U.S. embassy," she repeated for at least the hundredth time.

He said something in Arabic and the man behind Sara bowed slightly and left, closing the door.

"Sit," he said in English.

She blinked and looked around, spotting a chair against the wall beside the door. She'd have to pass by the desk to reach it. There was a phone on the desk, a few folders—one opened. Was that on her?

"I'm an American citizen. I wish to call the U.S. embassy. This has been a mistake that can be easily cleared up."

"Sit." It was clearly an order.

Moving to the chair, Sara sat gingerly on the edge. Gorgeous or not, his manners needed work.

He stepped behind the desk and fingered a sheet of paper in the opened file.

"You were arrested attempting to photograph a private dwelling—one which had posted signs warning trespassers away. You were trying to photograph members of the ruling family without permission. You carried no passport or other identification." He looked at her. "How did you get into this country and for what purpose?"

Sara swallowed. She needed to keep her father out of this mess if possible. She could imagine the result of his business negotiations if the world's press caught wind of the situation. It wouldn't be good.

"My passport and other identification are in my

room." She'd traveled light when heading out on assignment. A blessing or a curse this time?

"And that would be where?"

Dare she tell him? Would he be discreet, believing she meant no harm? His dark eyes held her gaze as if by merely looking at her he'd determine if she spoke the truth or not.

"At the Presentation Hotel in Staboul."

He tilted his head slightly. "First-class accommodations," he said, flicking a glance over her disheveled clothing.

She cleared her throat and tried to smile brightly. "I have a room there, with my family."

"And that family would be?"

Who was this man? His suit was the finest Italian cut. His pristine white shirt contrasting dramatically with the dark maroon tie. His hair was cut short, and he carried himself with an arrogant air. He looked sophisticated and totally out of place in this office.

And from the way the other man bowed before leaving, the stranger was apparently someone of rank in this country. How susceptible would he be to keeping quiet about her identity?

"If you'd let me make a call—"

He shook his head. "First, tell me who you are and then I'll consider it."

"I'm Sara K—Sara Kay. I'm a newspaper photographer on assignment. I was only trying to get some photos to show Americans what the sheikh's home looked like. Your ruling family's very secretive—especially since the death of sheikh Asim Kareef Riyad six months ago. We're curious, that's all. There's nothing sinister about it."

"Then why not request permission to make the photographs through normal channels?" he asked.

"I tried, no go."

"And did you not think there might be a reason for that?" His voice was hard, with an edge that set Sara's back up.

"Like what?"

"Privacy, perhaps?" he said softly.

"In America, once a family's in the public eye, their privacy's gone. The general public wants to know all about them."

"You're not in America."

Sara nodded, eyeing the phone. She wished she dare snatch it up and dial her parents. She hadn't a clue how to reach the hotel. And she knew this man would easily stop her if she made any attempt.

"Look, if you let me make one call, I can get this all cleared up. Or you might let me go. The other guys took my camera. I don't have the memory card, so no harm done. I'll promise not to photograph anything ever again. Can I go?"

Preferably with her expensive camera, but at this point, Sara'd be grateful to be allowed to leave.

He closed the folder with finality.

Her heart sank.

She wasn't going to waltz out of here on her own. She'd have to use her family's name, call on the influence of her father. She bit her lip.

Was there another way? Her father would kill her!

"Your actions have put into motion a chain of events that could have serious repercussions," he said slowly.

"From trying to take a few pictures?" she asked in disbelief.

"Perhaps you don't fully realize the situation. My country's in the midst of delicate negotiations with American business entities over oil reserves recently discovered here in Kamtansin. There are men in high positions in our government who do not wish to work with the Americans. The ministers are watching to make sure our country has the best representation. There are those who want the country to move into a completely different direction. The money the leases will bring will go a long way to improving the standard of living for all our citizens. Your actions jeopardize the entire negotiations."

Sara swallowed. "Please let me go," she almost whispered. "I wouldn't tell a soul."

"Too many people already know you're here and why. The charge is espionage. We do not take kindly to people flaunting our laws. You requested permission to photograph the family and were denied. How would you describe your actions?"

"I wasn't spying!"

He continued as if she hadn't interrupted. "The old guard would love nothing more than to prove to the world that we will not tolerate a flaunting of our laws and customs—especially by an American. They wish to make an example of you. It would add weight to our side of the negotiations as well."

Oh, great. This was the single biggest screw up she'd ever committed—and could ruin her father's business deal. She could already hear her mother.

"On the other hand, if negotiations are to continue, we dare not risk alienating the Americans by holding one of their citizens merely to make an example of her. If you truly work for a newspaper, I imagine the press coverage would be rampant."

She watched him closely, afraid to say a word.

Please decide on the don't-alienate-the-American side, she prayed, realizing the full impact of the situation.

She felt a little sick. She'd only been trying to get pictures for the paper—nothing sinister. She'd never envisioned causing an international incident.

And she certainly didn't want to jeopardize her father's negotiations.

The door opened behind her. She turned to see the man who'd brought her to the room. He spoke rapidly in Arabic. The man behind the desk nodded.

"Go, now," he said in English, turning back to the window deep in thought.

The guard walked to Sara and took her arm, pulling her to her feet.

"Wait," Sara said, pulling against the grasp the other man took on her arm. "Please, let me call the hotel. My father can vouch for me. He's Samuel Kinsale. He knows the sheikh!"

Two

Kharun froze at the words. The woman's father was Samuel Kinsale? The man he'd been working with for weeks in negotiating oil leases? He spun around and looked at her again.

Her bedraggled appearance didn't suggest the daughter of one of the world's most wealthy and powerful men, but two days in a local jail explained that. The prison facilities in his country weren't known for their lavish appointments.

Her honey-blond hair needed brushing, but it still looked soft as a woman's hair should. Her expressive gray eyes flashed and sparkled as every emotion showed in her face. Her clothes, if clean and pressed, would have been quickly recognized as top quality. He should have noticed that first thing.

But what was that story she gave about being a photographer? Was that a cover? Was she in truth acting as a spy, like Hamin and Garah claimed? Was she searching for a weakness in their side her father could exploit to hammer out a better deal?

Or had she blundered in where she had no business being?

"And what's the daughter of an American oil magnate doing spying on my family?"

"Your family?"

"I'm Kharun bak Riyad. That home you were trying to photograph belongs to my family."

"Oh, sheesh, I'm in deep trouble now!" she said with a groan. At least she was consistent, the older she got, the bigger the mistakes.

She looked at him closely. The few pictures she'd seen of the man in the last few months had been too distant and tiny for her to recognize him up close and personal. This was one of the people she'd hoped to photograph.

"You have made the situation a hundred times worse," he said.

He switched to his native tongue and told Jabil to return the woman to her cell. Watching as she protested, he let no expression show on his face. He'd become good at hiding his thoughts during negotiations. Never let the other person know his feelings was his motto. It stood him in good stead now.

As soon as they'd left, he turned back to the window. But he didn't see the oasis to the left with the soaring date palms, the green grass that flourished in the midst of the sandy desert or the drab houses of those who eked out an existence on the edge of the dunes. Nor did he see the endless desert beyond that stretched out to Morocco, wild and free and beckoning.

He saw instead the council chamber he'd left that morning. His uncle's handpicked ministers fighting against the men his father recommended for the council.

New regime against the old. Antiquated ways clashing against the hope of moving his country into the twenty-first century.

And smack in the middle came the daughter of the man he was negotiating with for oil leases that would enable the government to make the reforms his father so longed for.

He'd involved himself in the situation before he knew all the facts. Now others knew of his involvement. So the final decision would be his.

What to do with Sara Kinsale?

Both sides would be watching. His father had ruled the council for years, the old faction knew him. Now they watched to see he didn't sell out the country.

The newer ministers were wary about moving forward too quickly. He knew they questioned if he possessed the capability to represent their country in the oil negotiations. They'd trusted his father and transferred most of that trust to him. But still, they watched.

Their country was such a dichotomy—rich and modern in the cities, poor and underdeveloped in the desert. With the influx of funds the oil leases would provide, more amenities could be brought to the outlying areas—raising the standard of living for all.

Whatever he decided, he had to handle it discreetly and with great diplomacy. His years in business taught him all he needed. Now it was time to implement a strategy to get them out of this sticky situation.

He turned and reached for the phone.

Sara lay on her cot, wishing for a tiny bit of comfort. Lumpy and narrow, she wondered if it was designed to add to being incarcerated.

She'd played her trump card—given her father's name—and it hadn't helped. Maybe the oil leases weren't as important as she thought.

Or maybe the sheikh felt he held the trump card with her in jail. Maybe he'd use that to force her father into giving concessions.

She groaned, wishing she'd never started this chain of events. Why couldn't she find some job she liked and was good at? Was she destined to be a screw up all her life?

Or maybe a jailbird the rest of her life. Did people still disappear with no one finding out what happened to them?

For the first time since her arrest she considered the possibility of staying in jail for a long time. She shivered, not liking the prospect at all.

She closed her eyes—seeing Kharun bak Riyad. The top businessman dealing with her father, nephew of the chosen leader of this beautiful Arabian country. The son of the sheikh who recently died and who'd played an important role as adviser to the ruler. Things could not possibly get worse.

Restless with her thoughts, she sprang up again and began to pace the small space. If her lapse of good sense resulted in negotiations breaking down, her father might lose the deal—another company would obtain the oil rights.

A major contract going south because of her impetuousness.

What would the sheikh decide?

She tried to blank out the memory of that fluttering of interest in the man—personal interest. Was the desert heat getting to her? He was part of her assignment—photograph the elusive Sheikh Kharun bak Rijad. Let the women of America get a good look at one of the world's most eligible bachelors—heir to the fortune built by his father and enhanced by his own efforts. Dynamic businessman of this small country on the Mediterranean Sea. She'd now met the man, and worried even more that things would go south for her father.

She'd thought the assignment would be a snap, that she'd be able to sell the story and pictures and make a name for herself with the newspaper. She'd wanted the credentials of a job well done to help her move to a more reputable newspaper. One that delivered news and commentaries, not sensationalism.

Trying to ignore the twinge she felt every time she thought about the tabloid aspect of her job, she focused on the fact it was a step toward more serious photojournalism.

She remembered how she cringed when seeing the flashy headlines splashed across the different tabloids at the grocery store checkout stands.

Her impetuosity once again landed her in trouble. But this time, her father could also suffer. She'd paid little attention to his plans, more concerned with learning how to operate the fancy camera she'd bought for the trip and trying her hand at reporting news.

Her editor had changed the two articles she'd written beyond recognition by the time they hit the stands. She tried for the exploitive tone of the paper, but it proved impossible.

She really wanted to do this story—always hoping for the best—a human interest kind of story, nothing sensational.

Sara didn't want to be the one to bring disgrace on her father. All she'd ever wanted was to make him proud of her. Now this. She should have kept her mouth shut. She should never have told the sheikh who she was. Sara Kay was an unknown, no one would rally around to rescue her.

But the daughter of Samuel Kinsale? Her father would spare no expense to find her. And if he didn't like the way she'd been treated, he'd stop the negotiations in a heartbeat.

Pacing back and forth, she wished she could turn back the clock. Would she have done anything differently?

Not get caught, for one thing. But the only way to avoid that, if she had the last three days to do over, was to not attempt the photo shoot. She'd gambled her career on that. Gambled and lost.

The afternoon hours dragged. Another day gone and she was no nearer to getting back to her family—or even letting them know she was all right.

Kharun seethed with impatience and frustration. His calls gave him the information he needed—Sara Kinsale was indeed the daughter of the man he was dealing with. The youngest child of a very worried man who was quietly trying to locate his missing daughter.

Samuel Kinsale, too, was aware of the delicacy of the negotiations. And for the time being, didn't seem interested in upsetting the balance. But that would change if he didn't locate his daughter soon.

What would he do when he found out his daughter was in jail being held on charges of espionage?

Kharun's trusted adviser, Piers, suggested hiding her until after the signing of the oil leases. But Kharun didn't see that as a viable option. Keeping her whereabouts hidden from her parents for weeks or months would be needlessly cruel.

Garah Sonharh, leader of the old guard, was the most vocal in pushing for prosecuting her as a spy. Kharun hadn't spoken to him--holding off as long as possible as he mulled the situation over.

He'd heard of Garah's demands from Piers.

Once he spoke directly with his uncle's strongest minister, he'd be committed to whatever story they'd have to stick with.

Kharun's call to his sister hadn't helped. She'd sympathized, discussed the situation, then offered a bizarre idea for scraping through unscathed. Bizarre nothing—it was plain stupid from start to finish.

Damn! He rose from behind the desk and paced the narrow room, wishing he could get on his horse and ride out into the desert until the entire situation made some kind of sense. The freedom he enjoyed on the back of Satin Magic brought a soothing almost mystic release to tension and turmoil.

But his horse was at his summer villa by the sea, and he was here, fifty miles inland.

Besides, he didn't think Garah would take kindly to being ignored while Kharun went riding.

He smiled cynically. It didn't matter what he did, Garah didn't approve.

Nor did his aunt. Her choice would be choose another negotiator. He possessed the international business experience to know what to bargain for and to stand for his principles. His uncle trusted him as he'd trusted his father.

The bottom line—Kharun had the final recommendation regarding the oil leases. His uncle, the ruler of their country, continued to hold the utmost faith in him. He'd better do something soon before it all blew up in his face.

For the first time, he gave his sister's suggestion serious thought. It was a dumb way to muddle through a crisis, but might be the only way to save face all around. And it would make it very difficult for Garah to carry out his threat for an espionage charge.

He summoned Sara Kinsale.

She entered the room with her head held high. Jabil released her and bowed out, closing the door.

"I want to call the American embassy," she said again.

Kharun's lips almost twitched in amusement. She showed strength, he noted, beginning to notice other things about her. She was taller than the average height of most of the women in his country. And that honey-blond hair shone like a beacon. She'd stand out in a crowd. She carried herself proudly. The curves the khakis displayed were womanly and alluring.

He jerked his gaze back to her blazing eyes. Silvery when she was angry, a light gray when not. If she went for the bizarre suggestion, he wondered if he'd be able to gauge her moods by the color of her eyes alone?

"I have confirmed your identity. Your father's escalating his search for you. Pretty soon it'll be impossible to keep the situation quiet. Not that you'll mind, will you? Once a public figure, privacy's lost, correct?"

She narrowed her eyes as she gazed at him, obviously not liking her own words thrown back.

"I apologize for infringing on your family's privacy. Next time I'll make sure I have permission for a photo shoot."

"Next time?"

She shrugged, still standing defiantly in front of him.

All her makeup had long since worn off. Her cheeks glowed with natural color and her lips looked full and sweet.

Kharun frowned and looked away. He needed to make sure they both understood the proposal—and not get confused with some fantasies about the delectable femininity before him.

"I spoke briefly about the situation and the possible repercussions earlier," he began.

She nodded. "I didn't mean to cause problems."

"There may be a way out of this quagmire with a bit of acting on both our parts. Are you willing to hear my proposal?"

She nodded. Her shoulders relaxed a bit. Was she relieved to let him find a way out of the mess? If it didn't harm her father, she'd be up for anything that got her out of jail.

"I suggest we pretend to the world that we have known each other for some time. That your trip to visit with your family's merely a cover to see me. That we became secretly engaged and you were planning on surprising me with photos of my family's home as an engagement present."

She stared at him, not moving.

"Are you totally crazy?" she asked at last, almost exploding the words. "Engaged? As in get married to each other one day? No one in their right mind would believe such a thing! Where did you ever come up with such a ridiculous idea? I can't believe that's the best you can come up with. Aren't you supposed to be some hotshot businessman? This is your proposal? I can counter it in a heartbeat—let me go. I won't say a word. Make up something—like you imposed a heavy fine. I can't believe you can't think of a rational reason to release me without repercussions!"

He let her rant and rave for a couple of minutes, fascinated by her passion. Her eyes blazed, her breasts rose and fell as she drew in deep breaths. Her cheeks flushed with color. Would she look as enticing in bed?

Where had that thought come from? He had no intention of finding out. He was trying to get through this potential scandal without either side losing.

He held up a hand for silence. She closed her mouth and glared at him. He almost smiled at the picture she presented. However, now was not a time to get sidetracked.

"On the surface, I agree it does seem strange."

Hadn't he ranted and raved at his sister only a couple of hours ago protesting the very idea?

"But there's a hint of merit in the idea. Hear me out. If we have a personal reason for your taking pictures of forbidden areas, we can scrape through both the ministers' anger and the embarrassment you'd cause your father if his daughter was publicly prosecuted and condemned. An engagement would only be temporary—until the oil leases are signed. At that point, you can return home and we'll make a joint statement that there were too many differences to overcome."

She blinked and continued to study him.

"It'd never work," she said at last. "No one would ever believe you'd fall for me."

That caught him by surprise. "Why not? You're pretty and adventuresome—traits which would appeal to any man. We might have met in any number of cities we've both visited."

"Puh-lease. You're the nephew of the ruler of this country. Your own father was an important member of the council before his death. I'm the flaky younger daughter of an oil dealer. If it was my sister, Margaret, I could see it, maybe. She's sophisticated, successful and never puts a step out of place. You don't even want to *suggest* such a proposal with me."

For a second he wanted to agree with her. But it wasn't for real. Merely a mock engagement to keep scandal from rocking a still precariously run country. And, of course, to ensure the negotiations concerning their newly discovered oil reserves continued with no awkwardness.

"It would take very little on your part—pretend to be my fiancée, attend a few social events, stay at my place temporarily. You do have some acting skills, surely."

She shook her head. "Been there, done that. Didn't take."

"What?"

"I tried acting. I'm no good at it. The kindest criticism I received was that I don't fully embrace the character. The rest pretty much said I was a total flop."

"Have you had experience at being a fiancée?"

She shook her head. "Nope, neither pretend nor real. It wouldn't work, you know, but thanks for the thought. Can't you let me go?"

"It will have to work, I see no other way out of this without complications on one side or the other. The next best suggestion was to secret you away to another facility and play ignorant while your parents worry and search fruitlessly for you. Is that a better choice? Or are you ready for the repercussions that would arise out of being tried for espionage?"

He saw he'd hit home with his first comment. She didn't wish to worry her parents any more than he did. She knew what a trial would do to her father's negotiations. Would she agree to this ludicrous scheme now that he'd played that card? One way or another it was up to him to ensure the negotiations continued with a favorable result. Would she make it easier or harder?

"Only a fiancée, right? Indefinite marriage date. Still in the getting-to-know-each-other stage?" she clarified.

"Show only," he confirmed. Any elation he felt, he kept hidden. Maybe they'd brush through, after all.

They'd only have to pretend until the deal was finalized in a few weeks, a month at most.

"Okay, then, I guess I'll have to agree. Now can I make a call?"

Before Kharun responded, the phone rang. He answered it, his eyes never leaving Sara.

Dare he trust her to fulfill her part? Trust that once she left the jail she wouldn't flee the country to avoid the consequences?

Or would she hang around hoping to get those pictures that caused her everything earlier this week?

"Garah, here, Kharun. I've heard some interesting rumors about an American spy you're holding at the jail," the familiar voice said when Kharun picked up the phone.

"You need a better source for rumors, Garah. No spies here. A misunderstanding about a present my fiancée wanted to give me."

The pause was minuscule. "Fiancée? I had no idea you'd become engaged. Your uncle made no mention of this to me. When did this happen?"

"Some time ago. Out of respect for my father's recent passing and the grief in my family at his death, we elected to wait until a more suitable time to announce our betrothal. However, her zeal to capture the family home as a gift for me has changed our timing. We will let everyone in the family know tomorrow morning."

"Interesting, I didn't even know you knew Samuel Kinsale's daughter, much less found time enough for a courtship." Suspicion was evident in his tone.

Kharun remained silent. The less he told the old

manipulator, the less he needed to remember and deal with later.

Wasn't it interesting that Garah knew who Sara was. How had he found out? Kharun only found out himself a couple of hours ago when Sara told him.

"And when's the wedding?" Garah asked.

"We haven't set a date yet. We'll decide after both families learn of our engagement."

"Ah."

Kharun felt the hair on the back of his neck rise. He didn't trust Garah as far as he could throw him. What was the wily minister thinking?

"Perhaps you should consider setting the date sooner rather than later. It's one thing to excuse a flighty fiancée, yet engagements can be so easily broken, correct? It would be something else to forgive a dutiful wife."

Kharun heard the threat in his tone. And knew his sister's idea hadn't been foolproof. Was Garah calling his bluff?

"Perhaps you're correct. I will let you know when we decide on a date. In the meantime, Sara and I will be returning to the capital this evening if you need to reach me again."

He hung up and stared at the phone. The man suspected a cover-up. Of all the ministers, Garah pushed the hardest to hear other proposals for oil sales. Kharun refused to give him any ammunition to stall the current negotiations.

He looked at Sara. "The plan has changed. We'll marry immediately."

Three

S ara gazed out the limousine window, amazed at how fast things spun out of control. She longed to look at the man seated beside her, but didn't dare make eye contact, or give him any reason to suspect she was interested in him beyond his being the one responsible for rescuing her from jail.

Maybe there was still a way to salvage the situation with his wacky idea of getting married—no matter how temporarily.

The desert was cloaked in shadows, deep and mysterious as the sun set in the west. She'd caught a glimpse of an oasis when they'd left the jail. And the sight of a little child scantily dressed, staring at the costly vehicle as they pulled away, broke her heart.

Somewhere out there was his luxurious family home. The contrast between what she'd glimpsed before being arrested and the tiny child at the side of the road was outrageous. Sara knew the same divisions of wealth existed all over the world, but she'd been sheltered from it most of her life.

The meagerness of amenities in the area had been apparent--nothing like the bustling modern capital city.

How did the leaders resolve living with their own abundance when they were surrounded by destitution?

How had she wound up agreeing to his scheme? If her father knew where she was, he would have done anything to get her out. Still, if the charge of espionage was made, she feared the outcome. Was there an alternative to his outrageous proposal? Her mind spun trying to find a solution that would suit them both.

As they sped toward the coast, she reviewed her options. Not many, if her word was to hold. Which it would. Her actions precipitated the situation. If she could avoid a major scandal with no adverse repercussions to her father and his negotiations, it was important to do everything possible.

Yet the thought of sneaking away in the dark and catching a ride home on the next available plane held a lot of appeal. Once out of Kamtansin, what could they do to her?

Should she throw herself on her father's good nature and ask for help?

"It'll take at least forty-five minutes to reach Staboul City," Kharun said from her left. "And if traffic's bad, even longer to reach my home."

Sara glanced his way, startled to find his intense gaze focused on her. She felt a shiver of unease. He seemed to fill the ample space of the limo.

Upon entering the limousine, he'd closed the glass between them and the driver. They were cocooned in a world of two for the ride. She could smell his faint aftershave, spicy and masculine. She looked away, aware her heart rate had sped up a notch.

The car hit a pothole, jerked, shuddered and quickly recovered, but not before throwing Sara against his hard chest. She scrambled to regain her balance, even more aware of the differences between them. She was tired, dirty and shaking off the fear of the last few days. He looked as immaculate as he must have done that morning.

He inclined his head slightly. "One of the benefits of the oil leases would mean funds to repair our roads. Perhaps you should fasten your seat belt."

"And would the benefits also include helping people in villages like the one we just left?" she asked, pulling the belt across. She didn't want to wind up in his lap again.

"The outcome will allow us to do many things, including extending our education for all children, building new medical facilities, providing new jobs. It's my hope to bring my country from a nomadic past into the technological future."

Swallowing hard, Sara tried to focus on the words and not the strange sensations that sparkled through her hearing his voice. She felt as if he'd touched her, when there were at least twelve inches of space between them. The very air seemed to crackle with tension.

She looked away, at the growing darkness. The time to reach the city seemed like an interminable time to be cooped up with Sheikh Kharun bak Rijad. Though not as long a time as it would be if she went through with his crazy scheme to get married.

"I suggest we use the time until we arrive to get to know each other. If we are to pull this off, I need to know more about you than you tried to take illicit photos in a restricted area and are the daughter of Samuel Kinsale."

"Will we be able to pull this off?" She had her doubts. Though she'd do nothing to harm her father's situation, she was afraid her acting skills were far below what was needed to convince people she and this powerful man were in love. She wasn't even comfortable riding in a car with him. What would it be like to pretend devotion? To be touched by those strong hands, be caressed—

She shut down those thoughts. Taking a deep breath she tried for rational thought. Merely because the man beside her was the sexiest male she'd ever met was no reason to lose coherent thought. She'd need all her wits about her if she was to come through unscathed.

"Shall I begin? Hello, I'm Kharun bak Rijad." He held his hand out.

Reluctantly Sara placed hers in his, hoping for a quick, formal, means-nothing handshake. Did his comment mean he had a sense of humor? So far she'd seen no evidence of one.

His touch startled her. His hand was warm, firm, holding hers as if she was precious crystal. Tingling sensations danced on her nerve endings, causing her to catch her breath. She felt swept away to another level of existence, as if everything before was a prelude to this wondrous delight.

Snatching her hand free she tried to smile, but her facial muscles refused to cooperate. Her heart raced in her chest. Warmth infused her. She took a deep breath—

a mistake since it filled her with his scent. She scrambled for coherence.

"How do you do? I'm Sara Kinsale, youngest child of Samuel and Roberta Kinsale." She could have added classic misfit, but she had a feeling he suspected that already.

"Now where would we have met, Sara? Not here, this is your first visit to my country. Perhaps another locale to which your father has traveled frequently and I had an occasion to visit?"

"He's traveled all over Europe. I sometimes go with them. How about Paris?"

He appeared lost in thought for a moment, then nodded. "That'll work. My mother's from France and I visit there often. I've been twice in the last couple of years. I assume you were there sometime during that time span?"

She nodded. "I haven't lived with my folks since I left for college, but did travel with them a few months ago to Paris." She'd been between jobs and at loose ends. Shortly after she'd returned home, she'd landed the photojournalist position.

"So you graduated from college, which one?"

She named one of the famous Ivy League colleges, then frowned slightly. "Only I didn't graduate. I never could settle on a major."

"Photography and journalism not being an option?"

"Back when I was eighteen I planned to follow in my father's footsteps. I studied business administration for a while—but found it too heavily focused on math and economics. So then I thought about becoming an interpreter—my French is pretty good. That didn't take, either."

"So the next course of study was?" he prompted when she fell silent.

"Next I tried drama. I even had a role in one of the college productions. I didn't succeed beyond my wildest dreams. Actually I was a dismal actress. The reviews didn't even try to be kind. That's why I question how this plan of yours will work. How can I pretend to be your fiancée if my acting skills are nonexistent?"

"As my *wife*, you will be beyond questioning. As long as you can appear dutifully attentive when we are in public, there should be no problem."

Her heart skipped a beat, resumed with a rapid pace.

"I can't marry you."

"That was settled before we left the jail."

"I know you said we had to marry, but think about it—it's crazy."

He leaned toward her, his eyes hard as flint. "Listen well, Sara Kinsale. Your actions have jeopardized something important for my country. We aren't the richest country on earth, with a standard of living above all others. Poverty and disease affect a lot of our people. I want to improve the entire country and to do so we need an influx of cash. Your father's brokering an oil lease that will bring in that influx. It's the perfect solution and I will not have it destroyed by the flighty irresponsible actions of one woman. You will marry me, you will appear to be my dutiful wife in public and you will say nothing to anyone until that lease is signed, sealed and delivered. At that time, we can arrange a quiet annulment and you can return to America and resume your normal life."

"Yes, sir!" She tilted her chin. She was not intimidated by his words, but almost exhilarated. What was wrong with her? She should have been quaking in her shoes. Instead, her blood pounded in her veins, her senses were attuned to every nuance and she felt more alive than at any time in her life.

So he wanted marriage, did he? All right. She'd show him what being married to her would mean.

"So where did you go to school? What's your favorite color and how come you're not already married?" she asked.

She kept surprising him. It'd been a long time since someone had done that. For one moment when he challenged her he'd thought she'd quail under his glare. But that little chin came right up and she'd given a sassy reply. If they'd been standing he had no doubt she would have stood toe-to-toe with him, tilting that stubborn chin and glaring at him with silvery eyes.

Jasmine's idea was totally ridiculous, but the longer he lived with it, the longer he was around Sara Kinsale, the more it grew on him. At the very least, it wouldn't be a boring marriage—however short.

He almost grinned at the surprise he envisioned on his aunt's face when she met his future bride. His uncle's wife liked to think she ruled the family. While always courteous and polite, Kharun was ruled by no one— especially his aunt who would have been happy living in the early days of the last century.

There would also be the possible added bonus of

getting the country more firmly on his side. People always were drawn to the romantic, he thought cynically, wondering how they could put a positive spin on the situation--and counter the rumors Garah would be sure to spread.

"I attended St. Albans in England, then Harvard, finishing with a graduate degree of business at Wharton in Pennsylvania," he said as he became aware she was waiting for his response.

"Oh." She sat back in her seat, eyeing him with a hint of respect—the first he'd seen in her gaze. "So you're practically an American."

"Hardly. My favorite color is green."

Though silver might be moving up to the top spot.

"And why I have not married is none of your business. Neither have you. Do you want to tell me why?"

She opened her mouth and he almost held his breath, wondering what she would come out with. When she snapped it shut and shook her head, he was disappointed.

"Did you know green's the color most likely to be a favorite of geniuses? Are you super smart?"

He definitely questioned that, given his plan to follow his sister's crazy suggestion.

"Your favorite color?" he asked.

"Blue. Favorite ice cream's vanilla, boring, I know, but I love it. Favorite TV shows are always home improvement ones--any rendition that comes on. Favorite food's dark chocolate—made any way and every way it can be. I've been supporting myself since I left college. And I don't have any pets, though I always wished we could have had a dog."

"Do you ride?"

She nodded. "Horses? Finest lessons to be had. Do you?"

"Yes. I have a couple of Arabians. Maybe we'll find we have something in common after all."

"We don't need anything in common. This is temporary. How long do you think it'll take to sign that deal? If you sign soon, we don't even have to get married."

"I have no way of knowing how long it'll take. If everything goes smoothly, another few weeks. If we run into complications, it could take longer. We've already been in negotiations for four months."

"Four months! Good grief, what's the holdup? I mean, don't you read the terms, agree or disagree, hammer them out and sign the darn thing?"

"It's a bit more complex than that. And having an American spy thrown into the mix doesn't help."

"I'm not a spy," she said through gritted teeth.

"I would have thought a spy would be more adept at blending in, if nothing else."

He glanced at her hair, still fascinated by it. His fingers itched to test its softness. He wondered if he twirled a curl around a finger if it would cling.

"Your hair sets you apart from most of the people in the country. You would have done better to wear a hat or dye your hair."

"Look, I'll make you a deal. You stop referring to me being a spy and I'll do my best to be an adoring fiancée."

"Wife," he reminded her.

"Fine! Wife for as long as it takes to sign the blasted treaty."

His cell phone rang. Kharun tapped it and heard his sister's voice.

"So, what happened?" Jasmine asked with no ceremony.

"My fiancée and I are on our way to my villa as we speak. There's been a slight change in the plans, however. Garah Sonharh found out about our visitor and began to question our relationship. We will be married immediately."

Jasmine audibly gasped. "You're kidding. You're not going to actually *marry* the woman! Kharun, that's even more stupid than my original idea. An engagement's one thing—but *marriage?*"

"It's settled. We shall meet the rest of the family in the morning. Tonight would not be auspicious." He glanced at Sara, taking in the rumpled and stained clothing, the tiredness around her eyes, and the glare that met his gaze.

"I'm sorry I suggested the idea. You should listen to Piers, his idea made more sense," Jasmine said.

"We have settled the matter."

"You always were headstrong. Why not stick with the engagement and to hell with Garah? Or let her stay in jail. It's not worth risking your future."

"I'll take care of my future. I'll call you in the morning, Jasmine."

"I thought you were taking me to the hotel," Sara

said as soon as he'd disconnected.

"Perhaps I shall do that in the morning."

"In the morning? I want to go tonight!"

"Looking like you do? Wouldn't there be a question or two about where you've been and what you've been doing?" he asked silkily.

"I thought you were concerned about my parents worrying about me," she tried.

"My secretary has already phoned them to assure them you are well—and with me. What's more natural than lovers who haven't seen each other in months to wish to be reunited?"

"Lovers?" She almost squeaked the word.

He hadn't thought beyond the ceremony that would join them in marriage. He hadn't thought about the reality after their vows.

Now he considered how difficult it might prove to be to ignore this woman when she was living in close proximity.

Her turn of mind already intrigued him. Her blond, silky hair drew his gaze time after time. And he found himself deliberately saying things to annoy her to see the sparkle in her eyes.

She had passion in her. Would that passion carry over to bed? Would she be hot and wild and as captivating as Sheherazade?

For the right man, he had no doubt.

Did she even suspect the direction of his thoughts? Was she having similar ones?

"We're not lovers!" she said.

"We could be."

"In your dreams."

"Time will tell."

"Hold on a minute. If you think getting married gives you the right to share my bed, we need to talk about this some more."

"It does give me the right. Whether I exercise that right or not remains to be seen."

"I have some say in this."

"Of course. The same vows give you the right to my bed."

"Oh."

She leaned back in her seat, her eyes wide, staring into space as if she'd suddenly realized the full implication.

Kharun watched her in the dim illumination. She looked lost and lonely and stunned with the thought.

And imminently kissable.

His gaze focused on her lips, damp from her tongue, faintly pink and full. What would she taste like? How would she respond if he pulled her into his arms and kissed her? Could he spark all that passion and have it focused on him?

"You stay out of my bed and I'll stay out of yours," she said at long last.

"Shall we continue our briefing?"

He didn't agree to her suggestion. Had she noticed? Apparently not, she continued with a litany of likes and dislikes, of vignettes of family life and friends. He settled back to watch her, enjoying the play of emotions across her face. And he continued to fantasize about threading his hands in that silky hair and coaxing curls around his fingers.

Four

It was long dark when they arrived at his villa. A few miles outside of Staboul City, it hugged the sea. Seventeen acres of privacy, with a beach that he rarely used. It had been a legacy to him from his father upon his death. He'd offered his mother free access for her life and she sometimes resided with him for weeks at a time, only leaving when the memories became too much and she needed a change.

For a moment he remembered how happy his parents had been. Had his grandparents opposed the match? He'd never heard, but often wondered if they had approved of their son marrying a foreigner. Born in France, his mother grew up in Morocco. She loved the desert, loved the culture and adored his father.

His aunt had never fully accepted her sister-in-law. He had no doubts how she would react to his marriage to Sara. It was best done quickly. They could excuse the lack of celebration and ceremony to the untimely death of his father six months ago. His family was still in mourning.

"I smell the sea," Sara said.

"My house is on the beach. You can swim in the sea

every day if you wish. Make sure someone is around in case you get into trouble."

During her recital of likes and dislikes, she'd revealed how much she loved the ocean. If nothing else, she should be content living here until they annulled their marriage.

He'd made a quick call to his housekeeper before they'd left the jail requesting she make up a guest suite for his fiancée. She'd informed him of his mother's arrival. While he could have used another day or two before presenting Sara to his family, it wasn't all bad that his mother was already in residence. He'd need all the allies he could get to pull this off. Jasmine would help. Now he'd have his mother on his side.

If only his aunt would take a quick trip somewhere.

But life never ran smoothly. Look at the situation he was presently in.

"Wow, that's yours?" Sara gazed at the house, lit up from top to bottom.

"It is."

"It looks like a French villa or something on the Spanish Riviera, not Arabian."

"My father built it for my mother. She's French. It's a good thing you speak French. She'll love conversing in her native language. She learned Arabic, of course, and English, but I know she misses her first language."

"Maybe this isn't such a good idea. It's one thing to fool your ministers, but your mother?"

"Your parents, too."

She looked at him. "I thought I could at least explain—"

He shook his head. "Unwise. One wrong word and the entire situation would blow up in our faces. I'd lose whatever steps I've gained and the lease negotiations would shatter. Only you, me and Jasmine will know the truth."

"Jasmine's your sister. Why can't I tell someone in my family?"

"No."

The car slid to a stop before the large double doors. They stood wide and a woman dressed in a uniform stood quietly to one side.

"Let's see if your acting skills have improved since college days," he said as the chauffeur opened the back door.

Sara climbed out, stiff and awkward.

Kharun spoke in Arabic when he asked if Sara's rooms were ready and Aminna responded in the affirmative. His housekeeper was efficient and discreet. And loyal—having been with his parents long before he inherited her services along with the villa.

"Your mother has already retired to her rooms. I didn't know when you'd be home, so did not inform her of your guest," the older woman said.

"Well done, Aminna. Time enough in the morning."

He placed his hand in the small of Sara's back and urged her into the house.

"I'll take you to your room," he said in English.

Sara had the impression of space as they hurried down the hallway in the direction he indicated. She'd scarcely glanced into the entrance, or the rooms beyond, though all were lighted. The ceilings were high. The terrazzo floors were cool beneath her feet and the walls were white, adding to the feeling of limitless space. The hall itself was wide, with doors opening off it here and there.

She couldn't take it all in at the pace he directed. Or with the tingling that had begun when his hand touched her back. She could hardly walk a straight line.

Fatigue had to be the cause. She'd not slept well the last two nights. For one foolish moment, she wanted to lean into that hand, rest against the strong shoulders that were so temptingly near.

Realizing how dumb the idea was, she stepped out of reach, but the tingling awareness lingered.

"If you tell me which room's mine, I'll be fine."

He opened a door and stepped aside for her to enter.

The bedroom was like a fairytale setting. French doors opened onto a veranda. The breeze from the sea billowed the gauzy white curtains. The bed was huge, dominating one wall, with netting draped around it as if waiting to shelter a princess.

A small sitting area jutted out at one side. Beyond the bed a door stood open to a luxuriously appointed bathroom.

"A hot shower sounds wonderful," Sara said as her gaze skimmed across the furnishings. What a dramatic change from the cell she'd inhabited for two nights.

"I'll make sure Aminna has something brought in for you to wear," Kharun said. "Please ring if you need anything." He stepped back into the hall, closing the door behind him.

Sara almost danced across the room. It was heavenly—and a light-year away from the tiny, dusty cell she'd been in that afternoon. She went to the French doors and peered outside. Flowers bloomed near the terrace, a path led away—to the sea?

She turned back. Time enough tomorrow to go exploring. Right now, she wanted that hot shower!

Stripping as she walked, she headed for the bathroom. She closed the door behind her and in seconds stood beneath the hot spray, relishing the feel of the water slipping over her body. Slowly she washed her hair, soaped her dusty skin.

As the warm water caressed her skin, her tired, traitorous mind imagined Kharun's hands caressing her body in a similar fashion, following the curves, touching her breasts, learning every inch of her. The heat that built within at the rampant thoughts matched the heat of the water.

A cold shower would be better, she thought, shampooing her hair for the second time. She wanted all trace of her recent experience erased!

And she needed to spend her time thinking how to explain the situation to her father. Especially when he'd know she'd never met the sheikh before.

Giving in to the tiredness that swamped her, she shut off the water. The towels were luxurious—in keeping with everything else she'd seen so far, thick and soft. She wrapped one around her, used another to wrap her hair.

She gazed around the bathroom. Except for her underwear lying on the tiles, she had nothing to wear.

And she wouldn't wear them again until clean. Snatching them up, she hurried to wash them in the sink and hung them over a towel rod to dry. They'd be ready by morning.

Opening the door, she stepped into the opulent bedroom. Maybe the housekeeper had placed a nightgown on the bed.

Sara stopped short. Kharun sat in one of the chairs in the sitting area, looking completely at home.

She gripped the towel. It was tucked firmly against her, nothing showed—indeed, it covered her almost to her knees. But she knew she had nothing beneath but damp skin, and that made her feel extremely vulnerable.

She glanced at the trail of dusty clothes and wanted to snatch them up, so he wouldn't notice. But of course he'd had ample time to notice. How long had he been in her room?

He raised an eyebrow, letting his gaze travel from her wrapped hair, across damp shoulders, down the length of her.

Heat swept through her. Her heart began to pound. She couldn't take her eyes off him.

"What are you doing in here?" she asked, going on the offensive.

He rose and started toward her. His hand held a gossamer nightgown. "I brought you something to sleep in."

She stared at the delicate material, knowing it was as light and sheer as the curtains that billowed in the breeze. She raised her gaze to meet his, surprised by the heat she saw. Her heart raced. Mesmerized by the look in his eyes, she couldn't move. Couldn't utter a word. The fantasy in the shower played out in her mind. She wanted to slam the door shut on the images, but couldn't.

He came so close she could feel the heat from his body, see the fine lines around his eyes, smell the male scent mingling with that from the sea air.

For a moment neither moved. Then slowly he lowered his head, blocking out the room, blocking out everything except him.

When his lips touched hers, Sara gave a small sigh and closed her eyes. His lips were warm and firm, moving gently against hers.

She almost missed it when his arms encircled her, pulling her against his hard body. She was too busy wrapping her own arms around his neck; holding on as his kiss inflamed every cell. His embrace was hot and exciting as he moved against her with sensuous pleasure. Her body felt consumed with growing desire. She was swept away from the memory of recent events, away from anything she'd ever experienced. Swept away with the magic of his touch, of his taste, of his caresses.

When he ended the kiss, she clung. Her lids were so heavy, she had to force them open, gazing into the deep, dark eyes of the man who still held her.

"The first kiss is always awkward. Better to have it in private than before an audience," he said.

Releasing her, he stooped to retrieve the nightgown that dropped to the floor. He pressed it into her hands and then brushed her lips once with his thumb as if capturing some of the moisture to take with him.

Sara watched as he spun around and left. The slight

click when the door shut released her from the spell.

Dazed, she crossed slowly to the bed, sinking down on the edge, holding the nightgown against her breasts, feeling the softness of the material and the damp terry cloth of the towels.

The first kiss? Oh, Lord, there were going to be more?

Five

When Sara awoke the next morning, her first thought was of Kharun. Wouldn't that stroke his ego? But not in the way he might like. She'd spent a long time last night trying to figure a way out of this outlandish proposal of his. There had to be a way to scrape through without going through with marriage.

Last evening before she slept, Aminna had brought her soup and salad and a soothing pot of tea. Once finished, Sara slipped into bed, wishing for the oblivion of sleep. It proved elusive as she worried about today.

Her parents were the first obstacle. Or maybe Kharun's mother.

Would she meet the men who questioned their relationship today? Have to defend herself to them? Show the world how much she loved Kharun—a man she'd met less than twenty-four hours ago?

How about his sister or his trusted adviser, Piers?

She pulled the sheet over her head, wishing she could go back to sleep and not wake up until they signed the darn old leases. The day loomed ahead, overwhelming and terrifying. They'd never pull this off.

But the scent of the sea beckoned. Long moments

later she threw back the covers, rising to pad over to the open French doors. The veranda's pergola offered shelter from the morning sun. A narrow width of sunshine still warmed the tiles near the edge. She stepped out, feeling the coolness of the tile gradually warm beneath her bare feet.

The breeze swirled the nightgown around her and she raised her head, letting the air brush through her hair. She wanted to go swimming, splash in the warmth of the Mediterranean, forget for a little while the mess she'd made of things.

But she couldn't. She first had to face the day.

She turned and reentered her room. Her clothes were on the chaise lounge near the door—washed and neatly pressed. Sighing softly, she snatched them up and headed for the bathroom. It was time to face reality.

Dressed, hair brushed, and wishing for some makeup, Sara entered the hallway and walked toward the entryway. She heard the murmur of voices, the clink of silver against china. Following the sound, she reached the dining room. It faced away from the sea. The French doors in this room opened to a garden. Riotous flowers bloomed everywhere—bright yellows, rich reds, and a waterfall of white blossoms, all contrasting with the deep green of leaves.

The scent mingled with that of fresh-baked croissants and heavenly coffee.

Kharun sat at the head of the table an older woman to his right. She wore a fashionable dress of French design. The pearls around her neck and in her earrings looked to be worth a fortune. She caught sight of Sara and paused, coffee cup raised halfway to her lips.

Kharun looked up.

"Sara, I thought you'd sleep in longer or we would have waited." He rose and came to the doorway, capturing her hand in his. Raising it to his lips, he pressed a kiss upon her soft skin, his eyes catching hers—narrowed in warning.

"Good morning." The tone was intimate, the look one of possession and desire.

All resolve fled. What was it about this man that had her reacting like some teenager when the captain of the football team noticed her?

He switched to French. "May I present my mother, Angelique bak Rijad? *Ma mère*, this is Sara Kinsale, my bride-to-be."

She arose to join them and gave Sara a kiss on each cheek.

"*Enchantée, mademoiselle.* My son told me of your betrothal. I know you kept it a secret because of my husband's recent death, but such happy news deserves its time in the sun. It will lift the gloom that settles on our family. Welcome. You may call me Angelique."

Next to the two of them, Sara felt frumpy and awkward. She wished she had something to wear beside the khaki safari outfit she'd thought so dashing only a few days ago.

"I am happy to meet you," she replied in French. At least she'd get some practice out of her expertise in the language.

Kharun seated her at his left and summoned Aminna to bring a new pot of coffee.

"Tell me all about this whirlwind courtship. I was beginning to worry about my son. He has been so consumed with business since his father put him in charge. Now I'm pleased to know he's also taking time to assure his future and that of the family. You have brought joy to my heart."

Sara smiled awkwardly, feeling guilty as sin at their deception, grateful when Aminna arrived with the coffee. She stalled, making a great to-do of preparing the beverage to her liking. Please let something happen to deflect the inquisition, she prayed. She looked at Kharun for help. He got them into this particular situation, he could get them out.

Despite her worry, breakfast proceeded without a hitch. Kharun did indeed get them out of the awkwardness, regaling his mother with the most fantastic tale of how they met. Sara listened spellbound, hoping she could remember every word in case she was asked. It'd prove smoother sailing if their stories matched.

By the time breakfast was over, Sara almost believed the fantasy herself—how they met in Paris, fell in love on the Rue de Calais, danced until dawn on the Left Bank, and learned more about each other strolling in the gardens of the Tulieries.

"I'd planned to visit for a while," Angelique said. "Now I will move immediately to Jasmine's apartment. You two will wish to be alone. Especially if you cannot take a proper honeymoon at this time. Kharun explained that once the oil deal is done, he'd be able to take time. You are very understanding to allow the delay."

Sara blinked, her gaze moving to Kharun. What had

he been telling his mother before she arrived? She smiled, wondering what she should say. She hadn't been a good actress when she had lines to memorize. Improvisation was even more difficult!

"We would not cut short your visit, Mother," he said.

"Nonsense, I remember how your father and I were—" Tears welled in her eyes and she blotted them with her linen napkin. She pushed back her chair. "Excuse me. I will instruct one of the maids to begin packing immediately." She left the room almost at a run.

"She should stay," Sara said, looking after her. "It's not like she'd interrupt anything."

"She and my father had a passionate love affair from the moment they met. I suspect she considers our situation similar. It's the only way she would understand an immediate wedding."

Having experienced one of Kharun's kisses, she had no trouble instantly imagining them in a passionate embrace. They would ignore the world around them, caught up in the moment of excitement, touch, feelings and passion. What would it be like to be in love with this man?

But what he'd said suddenly hit her. "*Immediate* wedding?"

"The sooner the better. Are you almost finished?"

She gulped the last of her coffee, blotted her lips with her napkin and laid it neatly on the table. Thoughts about Kharun were the last thing she needed. If she was to get through this charade, she needed her wits about her—not daydreaming.

"I'm ready," she said.

"It's early yet. We have time."

"It's never too early at a hotel—they're open twenty-four hours."

"What do you mean?"

"You said you'd take me to the Presentation Hotel this morning. I'm ready."

"After our wedding." He looked at his watch, then met her stunned gaze. "Which I scheduled for ten. I think Jasmine has found you a suitable dress."

"*What?*"

He rose and left before she could formulate a coherent sentence. She followed him from the room with her gaze, stunned at the announcement. He couldn't have been serious! She couldn't marry him *this* morning. Weddings took tons of planning. Invitations and fittings and... and...

She didn't know what else, having never married before. But she didn't think any one could plan a wedding with no more than twelve hours' notice.

And without telling the bride first.

She jumped up, intent on finding him and telling him why they couldn't marry today. A few hours away from that awful jail and she'd begun to think of alternative scenarios that would let them off the hook. She had to find Kharun and offer different ideas before this one got out of hand.

As she walked into the entryway searching for her reluctant host, the front door opened and a petite, slender young woman entered, wearing a lovely rose-colored silk suit. Accompanying her was a tall man dressed in a chauffeur's uniform carrying a garment bag over one arm. The woman's dark hair gleamed in the sunshine looking almost blue-black. The two of them stared at each other for a moment.

"You must be Sara," the woman said in flawless English.

"Jasmine, I presume," Sara guessed. The woman looked like a small, feminine version of Kharun.

The sunny smile that broke out was a surprise. Jasmine nodded, studying Sara. "No wonder my brother said yes to that crazy spur-of-the-moment idea."

"It'll never work," Sara said.

"If Kharun says it will, it will. I have brought your wedding dress." She flicked a glance to the man standing beside her. "Which room did Aminna give you?"

"Down there," Sara indicated. "But—"

Jasmine took the garment bag from the chauffeur and dismissed him. She turned to head for Sara's room.

"Quickly, you need to try it on. It wasn't easy to get something in your size on a moment's notice. Kharun called me at seven this morning asking if I would pick up a wedding dress. Doesn't he know most boutiques don't open before ten? Silly question, of course he doesn't. Let's see if this fits."

Sara followed, feeling swept away by a whirlwind.

Twenty minutes later Sara stared at her reflection in the floor-length mirror. Everything was spinning out of control. She hadn't found Kharun, but had been rushed along with Jasmine, coerced into trying on the gown.

The creamy-white dress fit as if it'd been made especially for her, lacy and elegant—suitable for cocktails, a trip to the theater, or a morning wedding. The shoes were a size too big, but Jasmine stuffed cotton in the toes. They were low-heeled enough to walk in.

Sara's blond curls encircled her head like a soft cloud. The light touch of makeup Jasmine brought enhanced every feature, deepening the mysterious look of her eyes, bringing a hint of a blush in her cheeks—making her look almost like a bride.

What would Kharun think?

At least she looked one hundred times better than when he'd first met her—when he'd made his proposal. Surely he could find no fault with the end result.

Slowly, Sara smiled. She liked how she looked. Maybe people wouldn't wonder what he saw in her. Maybe they could pull this off. For the sake of her father she had to try.

Jasmine met her gaze in the mirror, her expression solemn. "Bring no disgrace on my family. Do no harm to Kharun. Do you understand?"

Sara raised her chin and glared at Jasmine. "I would never do that. Nor bring disgrace to my family—isn't that the entire reason for this charade?"

In those short words, reality returned. She was not a blushing bride going to exchange vows with the man she loved. She was entering into a marriage of convenience—not even her convenience—to rectify a mistake. She would not compound it by forgetting for one second why the marriage was taking place.

Taking a discreet peek at her watch, she realized if the wedding was to begin at ten, she had no time to find Kharun and propose her alternative suggestions. It didn't matter, she knew he'd never have accepted her ideas. The time for deciding had long passed.

This could work. Once the leases were signed, they'd get an annulment and go their separate ways. She could do this. It was only for a few weeks.

Kharun left nothing to chance. He arranged for Samuel Kinsale and his wife to attend the ceremony. To do less might raise suspicions. But he timed their arrival to be only a few minutes before he planned the ceremony to start. They could visit with their daughter after she was legally his wife.

His mother and sister, of course, would attend. His most trusted adviser, Piers. He did not send an invitation to his aunt and uncle. He wouldn't risk their disrupting the ceremony before it could begin. Being a family in mourning helped. A quiet ceremony would be all people expected.

He hoped this charade worked. He'd do his best to see to it!

Promptly at ten, Samuel Kinsale and his wife Roberta arrived. Angelique greeted them and led the way to the garden nearest the sea. She answered their questions as best she could, but Samuel wasn't satisfied. He and his wife had no indication their youngest even knew Kharun, much less planned to marry him, until that morning when Kharun had phoned. And the explanations had been hasty and brief.

Angelique told him what she knew and urged them to await to question Sara until after the ceremony.

The garden was the perfect setting for a quiet, family wedding. Kharun cynically reviewed everything from his place at the doorway. On the surface the locale presented as romantic a picture as he could devise. As long as no one questioned them closely, or challenged anything, it should go off without a hitch.

Kinsale remained a question mark. He hoped the man would listen to his mother and not question Sara until after the ceremony.

Sara was also an unknown. Would she go through with the bargain? Or would she defect at the last moment—thus giving Garah and his associates a weapon to use in their determination to halt progress?

Jasmine hurried down the hall and smiled uncertainly at her brother.

"She's as ready as I can make her. Good luck, brother. I still think an engagement would have worked."

"Sit with mother, she's a bit overwhelmed."

"I don't blame her. How's the bride's family taking it?"

He glanced out to the garden, frowning slightly. "Better than I expected, actually, though her mother looks shell-shocked. Her father put up a fuss when he first arrived, but seems content with waiting to talk to Sara later. I wonder if he'd already heard the rumors? He would appreciate the need for such a step."

"Maybe they're glad to get her off their hands," she murmured as she slipped past on her way to join the others.

He turned and waited until he saw Sara walking down the hall. For a moment Kharun forgot they were entering into a mock marriage for business necessity. His bride appeared entirely different from any other time he'd seen her—including earlier that morning.

He almost caught his breath. She looked shy, virginal and breathtakingly lovely. There would be few questions asked when his uncle's ministers saw her. They'd immediately conclude the reasons why he was marrying her—for her looks, her mind and her background.

"Are my folks here?" she asked, stepping up to the doorway.

"Everyone's gathered in the garden. Are you ready?"

She hesitated a moment, then nodded, reluctantly. "As I'll ever be. Are you sure there isn't another way?"

"I'm sure." He held out his arm.

She took his elbow, gripping tightly. "Shouldn't my father walk me down the aisle?"

"It's a very informal wedding—only immediate family. I don't think we need to stand on protocol."

"Or you don't trust me alone with him before?" she whispered as they stepped into the sunshine.

She'd given her word of honor. He might not think much of it given the circumstances, but it meant a lot to her. She smiled at her parents, but continued to hold on to Kharun. She'd set this in motion, she'd see it through. Better her family thought she was rushing into marriage than to learn the truth. When it didn't last, they probably wouldn't be surprised.

Maybe one day, after her father finalized the deal, she'd tell them the whole story.

But not today. Today she was getting married in a lovely garden, with the Mediterranean Sea in the background, to a man who could have been a dream come true—but might prove to be her worst nightmare.

Six

Sara knew the day would forever be etched in her memory as a series of sketches—from the fragrance of the flowers surrounding her while she gave her vows, to the hot, demanding kiss Kharun'd given to seal their marriage, to the bewildered look of her mother when she turned to hug her. Both her parents had pulled her aside as soon as the short ceremony ended and questioned her about the totally unexpected wedding.

Sara's history of impetuousness stood her in good stead. They were not surprised by anything she did anymore, so accepted the fact she and Kharun had decided to marry after a whirlwind courtship. Her mother asked questions galore, but Sara put her off, promising to visit soon and let her know all the details. Her fingers firmly crossed behind her back she hoped the need for the charade would end before her mother cornered her alone.

The wedding lunch had been extravagant—as if the staff had had weeks to prepare instead of less than twelve hours.

The conversation had proved stilted and awkward as Kharun's family, except for Kharun and Jasmine, did not speak English, and Samuel and Roberta Kinsale didn't speak Arabic. Her father had a limited command of French, so there was limited conversation between him and Angelique.

It had been a strain—pretending to be a blushing bride, all the time aware of the man beside her. Of his fingertips brushing against hers, which sent jolts of electricity shooting in every direction. Of the intensity of his gaze—which the others had taken as devotion, but Sara knew was more of a warning to keep their deception going.

The trip to the hotel to gather her clothes later that afternoon had been accomplished with no fuss. Kharun never left her side. She knew he didn't trust her, but to anyone else, it looked as if he were a devoted bridegroom who couldn't bear to spend time away from his beloved.

The oddest memory was of the confused feelings she'd experienced when Kharun had bid her goodnight and left her in the middle of the living room.

By then everyone had left—including Aminna. Only she and Kharun remained in the villa. Aminna would return in two days—it was all Kharun had asked for a honeymoon, alluding to a longer one when the demands of his time were less immediate.

She might as well be alone in the world, Sara thought as she listened for some sound. Once his footsteps faded, she heard nothing except the soft soughing of the sea breeze and the rustle of the curtains as they moved with the wind.

She went to her bedroom and closed the door.

Within minutes she was nestled in bed, with a magazine she'd seen earlier in hand. But her thoughts were not on the pages.

She'd never thought about getting married—not for years. And certainly not to prevent an international scandal. But being alone in a big bed was never her fantasy for her wedding night. She was disappointed Kharun hadn't spent more time with her. Sending away the staff had been brilliant—no one around to see they were not the lovers everyone suspected.

But for a moment, she almost wished he'd taken advantage of his right to share her bed.

Shocked at the idea, she clicked off the light, letting the magazine slide to the floor as she scooted down on the mattress. Her last thought as she finally drifted to sleep was that she hoped the business talks would conclude soon.

Sara awoke early the next morning, having slept better than she expected. She dressed quickly in a sun dress she'd brought and wandered out onto the veranda. The sun was already warming the day. The sea sparkled beneath its rays, looking cool and inviting. She followed the path that led through the gardens to the beach. A quick glance around assured her she was alone. The servants wouldn't return until late tomorrow afternoon. Where was Kharun? Still asleep?

The image of him in a bed flashed into her mind. He'd need a big bed. Would he sprawl across it, taking up all the room, or keep to the edge as if ready to leap up in a second's notice?

Did he sleep in anything?

She doubted it.

The thought brought tantalizing new images to mind. Trying to block them out of her mind, she opened the low gate on the path that led to the sand. Sara kicked off her sandals and walked on the hot surface. Running quickly to the water's edge, she almost danced in relief as the cool sea lapped at her feet. Looking left and then right, she saw she was totally alone. She tried to imagine such a pristine location being empty in America—impossible. Every time she'd gone to the beach, she'd had to share it with families and couples and teenagers. Today's solitude was blissful.

She walked along the water's edge.

When she reached a notice board, written in Arabic, she turned around. Maybe that was the edge of Kharun's property. She'd ask, but in the meantime, she was growing hungry. Longingly, she gazed at the water. She wanted to swim, but knew she needed someone else around to be safe. Maybe later. Turning, she headed for the villa.

She brushed her feet off when she reached the gate and donned her sandals again. Walking through the gardens, she wondered if it would be okay to pick some of the blossoms to carry to her room. They were so lovely and fragrant, she'd enjoy them where she could see them.

She entered her bedroom, crossing to the hallway. It was the only way she knew to reach the dining room. Maybe she'd spend some time today exploring the villa. If she had to live here for a few weeks, she might as well know the layout.

When she reached the entryway, a loud knock sounded on the door. Sara hesitated. Should she see who it was or wait for the maid?

There was no one else around.

The knock sounded again.

Sara opened the door and saw an elderly woman dressed all in black, her gray hair pulled tightly back in a bun. Her skin was wrinkled, no makeup softened the aging process. Her eyes snapped when she looked at Sara. Her gaze ran from head to toe and then back.

Beyond her was a huge old car. The chauffeur stood near the front, watching the scene impassively.

The woman said something.

"I hope you speak English or French, because I don't speak Arabic," Sara said. Then repeated the sentence in French.

The woman responded in that language.

"The wife of a sheikh should at least speak his language," she snapped. "Are you going to invite me in?"

"Please," Sara said, stepping aside, wondering who in the world the woman was.

"I suppose it's too much to expect my nephew to inform his uncle and me when he weds. That's so like him to ignore family in his pursuit of his own ways. I have told Hamsid, but does he listen? No. Just like a man!"

Sara watched the woman—obviously Kharun's aunt. Had he mentioned her to Sara? She didn't remember an aunt. How close were they if he didn't invite her to the wedding?

"Well, where is he?" she snapped, glaring at Sara.

"Kharun?" Sara ventured.

"Who else?" The woman peered at her as if she were stupid.

Sara looked around, hoping inspiration would strike. She knew the circumstances surrounding their marriage were top secret. But everyone would expect a new wife to know where her husband of less than twenty-four hours was.

"Um, I'll go get him," she said. "Would you like to wait—"

"I'm not going traipsing throughout the place to find him. Where are the servants?"

"They were given a few days off. So we could be alone."

"Then hurry."

Sara turned toward the dining room almost skipping in her haste. She hoped she could find Kharun and prayed he hadn't left. What would she do if she had to return and tell the woman he'd gone out?

How many rooms did the house have she wondered five minutes later. She'd tried every door she'd come across. Some of the rooms looked lived in, others like showplaces. But all were empty of human life.

Sara stopped and wanted to scream. The impatient woman was waiting. She had no idea where her husband was nor what she to do next. How dare he put her in this position!

Slowly she retraced her steps, heading for the entryway. If she had any luck, the woman would have tired and left.

The sound of voices alerted her to the fact Kharun

had found their guest. Thank goodness.

She drew a deep breath and hurried to join them.

Kharun and his aunt didn't notice Sara slipping into the room, they were too busy arguing. She didn't understand a word, but she understood the anger in their tones, and the hard glares they exchanged.

Suddenly Kharun saw Sara. He stopped talking and smiled.

Sara's heart caught then turned a slow, lazy somersault. It was the first time she'd seen him smile at her. She'd thought him handsome when she'd first seen him, but his smile almost stopped her heart. The man should be registered as a lethal weapon and a warning issued to all females under the age of ninety-eight!

Caught in his gaze, she strolled toward him, her skin tingling with awareness and the potent attraction any woman feels around a stunningly masculine male.

He wasn't wearing a suit, she noticed dimly. His shirt was loose, buttoned only partway up, exposing a wedge of broad tanned chest sprinkled with dark hair.

His hair was mussed as if he'd run his fingers through it while working. Or as if tossed by the sea breeze. Had he walked along the shore today as well?

His trousers were loose and he was barefooted—his feet planted firmly on the floor as if boldly staking his claim and asserting to the world he was totally male—ready to take on all comers. She swallowed hard, amazed to realize this man was her husband.

"Ah, Sara, I wondered where you were," he said in English. His voice was sultry, sensuous. His eyes caressed her. His hand reached for hers, drawing her closer, his fingers tightening in warning as he pulled her close enough she felt the heat pouring from his body.

Mesmerized, she could not say a word, but her senses seemed to kick into overdrive. Every nuance was clear, dazzling. His fingers holding hers were warm and strong. His eyes tried to convey a message, but she wasn't sure what he wanted.

Until he swept her into his arms and kissed her.

She didn't know this man, wasn't sure she even liked him. His kiss meant nothing—merely show for an audience of one.

One touch, however, and she felt afloat on a sea of sensation and delight. Bright colors danced behind her lids. Her blood seemed to heat until she wondered if it would evaporate. Her senses swam with delight, with shimmering pleasure.

When his tongue stroked her lips, she parted them. When it danced in her mouth, she met each foray with a caress of her own. When he deepened the kiss, she pressed against the length of his hard body, shocked with the reaction she was causing. But it wasn't enough. She wanted more.

A harsh exclamation behind her slowly penetrated. Kharun eased back, breathing hard as he gazed down into her eyes, his own shuttered and impossible to read.

He placed his arm on Sara's shoulders and turned her into his body, still holding her as he spoke in French, "What did you expect, Aunt? Sara and I haven't seen each other for months. We married and don't have time for a honeymoon. We'll make our own, here and with every moment we can spare."

"I do not understand this. Take your honeymoon, there's nothing that cannot wait."

"You forget the oil leases I'm negotiating."

"Bah, you're more than foolish if you think you will get the ministers' full approval. Your uncle indulges you beyond what is acceptable. But the treaty is not ratified yet."

"We have discovered a new reserve, a huge one, that will enable us to make deals for years to come. The new influx of cash will enable changes, improvements. Bring us into the twenty-first century," he said in Arabic, explaining what she already knew.

"Your father—"

"Unfortunately he's dead. Out of deference to our mourning, Sara and I had a quiet ceremony yesterday. Mother and Jasmine represented our family. Sara had her own parents present. When our mourning time is over, we'll have a public reception and you may formally welcome Sara into our family."

The woman glared at Sara. She spoke again in Arabic. Kharun tightened his hold, his eyes blazing with anger. He responded in the language then disengaged himself from Sara and headed for the front door.

In a very polite voice, he turned and bid his aunt farewell.

When he shut the door behind her, he spun around and looked at Sara.

"That went well."

"That went well?" she exclaimed. "I didn't understand a word of what she said, but I didn't need to. Her tone spoke volumes!"

"Ah, but she never once suspected this as a coverup. She deplored my choice of brides, warned me to keep a tight rein lest you ruin us all, and railed against me for defying the ministers who have more experience in deciding things than I do. But not once did she act as if she didn't believe the marriage is real."

Seven

"If she thought about it for two seconds, she might have," Sara mumbled, annoyed Kharun seemed so pleased with himself.

"Why?" He focused his attention on her.

Sara almost shivered, the memory of that hot kiss sending heat washing through her. He was an intense man and when he turned that intensity on her, she felt like she was the only person in the world.

"I didn't know where you were, nor how to find you. If you hadn't wandered in on your own, I'd be making up some sort of excuse as to why a bride didn't know where her bridegroom was twenty-four hours after the wedding!"

He nodded. "Good point. Come with me, I will show you around the villa and how to use the intercom system. When Aminna's here, she can always find me. Or one of the maids can."

"She'll be back tomorrow. If we don't have any more unexpected guests, I don't need a tour." She couldn't explain her reluctance to spend time with Kharun. They meant nothing to each other, yet he kissed her as if she were his passion. And she responded like a firecracker.

False passion—he turned off the charm instantly when they were alone. She couldn't help responding even when he wasn't acting. Even standing there had her fantasizing about things that could never be. He made no effort to entice her.

To him their arrangement was designed to keep scandal from tainting his negotiations.

He didn't have to do anything but stand there and she was captivated.

She looked away, trying to get her wayward emotions under some sort of control.

"Come and see the villa, anyway. My mother decorated it over the years. I urged her to take some of the furnishings or paintings for her own apartment when she left after my father's death, but she says the memories become too strong and too sad."

For one foolish moment, Sara wished he'd held out his hand when urging her to come on the tour. She would love to slip her hand into his to feel his strength, to feel anchored. To revel in the shimmering waves of tingling awareness that would shoot up her arm at his touch. To fantasize a bit more before reality returned.

She frowned as she stepped toward the arched hallway. Where had that last thought come from? She didn't want to be anchored and she didn't need fantasy in her life.

She was a free spirit—hadn't her parents lamented that fact for years? She still had to make her way in the world and show her parents she could accomplish something worthwhile as her siblings had.

"Do you have my camera, Kharun?" she asked as they walked down the corridor opposite the one that led to her bedroom.

"Planning to complete your assignment?" he asked warily.

She flushed slightly. "No. But it's an expensive piece of equipment that I'd like to have back."

He paused by an open doorway. It was an office, set up with two computers, an enormous desk, and rows of bookshelves along one wall. French doors opened to the wraparound veranda and allowed the cool breeze to waft in.

"It's in here," he said, pointing to the desk.

On the corner sat the camera.

She stepped warily inside the office and went to the desk to pick it up. She checked the exposure indicator—reset to zero.

"The card was confiscated," he said, leaning against the doorjamb.

"I expected nothing else. May I have another one?"

"To do what?"

"Exactly what I asked myself earlier," she said, swinging around and leaning against his desk. It was easier to face him with the width of the office between them.

"What am I to do all day?"

"What do you do at home?" he returned.

"I have a job, so I show up at the office, scout around for new stories. There's shopping to do, friends to meet, laundry, household chores."

He raised an eyebrow. "Do you cook?"

She nodded.

"Since Aminna isn't here, maybe you'd like to prepare some food for us."

"I don't suppose sheikhs learn to cook."

"Your assumption's flawed. I was on my own several times—when away at school. I can cook enough to get by when a restaurant isn't convenient."

"And a restaurant isn't convenient today?" Sara asked.

He slowly smiled and shook his head.

Her heart turned over. Her knees grew weak and she thought she'd have to learn to breathe all over again. She'd already thought he was a striking example of alpha male, dominating any situation he was in, but when he smiled, he was devastating. If he didn't already have a calling, she knew he'd be an instant hit in Hollywood.

She tried to hide her reactions.

"So that gives me something to do today, what about the rest of the time while you're off negotiating oil leases and running a company?"

"We can work on that. It may only be a matter of weeks. Pretend you're on vacation. Enjoy the beach. You said you love the sea. Maybe go shopping. Come, I'll show you the rest of the villa and then you can prepare lunch."

She picked up the camera and looked around the room. "This is command central, I suppose?"

"It's my home office. As you know the business is headquartered in Staboul. But when I'm not there, I need instant communication and access. Unless I'm present, please do not enter this room." His voice hardened with the last command.

She tilted her chin and glared at him.

"I told you once before, I am not a spy. Anyway, I don't speak Arabic, so any secrets you had would be safe from me. I have no interest in your dumb old office."

She swept toward him with as much dignity as she could muster beneath the smoldering anger. What would it take to convince the man she was only a sometimes inept novice reporter for a second-rate U.S. tabloid and not a sexy, conniving spy?

Not that the sexy spy role didn't have advantages, she thought as he stepped aside to allow her into the hall. Weren't sexy spies notorious for seducing secrets from lots of men? For a moment Sara wondered if she had the capability to seduce Kharun.

The tour took more than an hour. She was impressed with the comfort level of the villa despite the antiques and costly items that predominated. The paintings on the walls were from famous impressionists, Renoir and even some modern ones.

Her favorite room was the one where Matisse paintings dominated an entire wall. She knew she'd come back on her own to soak up the ambience and enjoy the paintings.

There were formal rooms, a quiet little sunroom, guest rooms for both family and visitors. Even an exercise room tucked in a back corner. On the far side of the villa was a pool, surrounded by fragrant flowering shrubs, which provided privacy.

"Why have a pool when the Mediterranean Sea's at your doorstep?" she asked when they entered the pool area.

"Some people prefer artificial to natural." He shrugged. "Here we have both. You're free to use either—provided you don't go swimming alone."

"Who would go with me?"

"If I am available, I will go. Otherwise Aminna or one of the maids or gardeners can watch to make sure you don't get into trouble."

"Afraid I'll swim away?" she asked lightly.

"No, Sara, afraid solely for your well-being. It isn't safe to swim alone."

She nodded, suddenly touched he'd extend his concern to her well-being after the trouble she'd caused. He was right, it was unsafe to swim alone.

Kharun ended the tour in the kitchen. Sara stared in amazement. "You must entertain a lot," she murmured, taking in the huge stainless-steel refrigeration unit, the industrial-size gas range, the two huge ovens and three microwave ovens. The counter space would provide enough room to cater a seven-course meal for fifty.

"My parents did a lot of entertaining. I don't do as much. Though now that we are married, I wonder if it will become expected."

"No."

"No?" He looked at her. "Why not?"

"I'm not good at parties," she said quickly. "Besides, we won't be married that long. No one would expect us to entertain."

"Why are you not good at parties?"

"I never know what to say to people. We've been involved with big events my whole life. You must know that most business deals are often dealt with at social functions. I never told my father, but I hate going to them. One wrong word and world peace as we know it could end."

Kharun laughed out loud.

Sara watched him, fascinated. Her lips twitched, but even his laugher couldn't erase the awkward feelings she got when faced with a roomful of strangers.

"It's not funny," she said.

He came to stand next to her—too close. She wanted to step away. She could feel the heat from his body as it seemed to envelop her, smell the scent from his skin that had her wanting to toss her camera to the floor and draw an enticing finger along the swell of his muscles to test their strength, taste him again.

She swallowed and stood her ground, hoping her pounding heartbeat wasn't evident to the astute man now staring down into her eyes.

"It's not funny, I apologize for laughing. But any faux pas you might make at a reception or dinner would scarcely end world peace. If you are uncomfortable, we won't entertain."

She blinked. That was totally unexpected.

"It's your home, if you wish to entertain, I'll do my best. Please understand I'm not so great at it. Now, Margaret, she shines at events like that. She knows exactly what to say, who're the most important people in the room, what the latest rumors are and how to defuse any awkward situations."

"Margaret—is she your sister?"

Sara nodded. "The attorney," she said flatly.

"Ah, I remember now, the attorney and the physicist and the… photographer."

"Photojournalist, this week."

Unless her boss had already fired her. She hadn't reported in for a week.

She looked at Kharun, trying to gauge his reaction if she asked to use the phone.

"I probably should let my office know what's happened."

He shrugged. "If they are any kind of newspaper, they already know. My office released news of our marriage this morning. I have cut off the phones to make sure we are not disturbed by reporters. My advisers will handle the world press."

"Oh. It must be nice to have a legion of people ready to do your bidding," she said.

He smiled as if amused by her comment. "It is. Lunch?"

Glancing around the room again, Sara nodded. She placed her camera on the edge of the counter and started opening cupboard doors, looking for something to start with.

"So I join the legions, here for your bidding."

"Unless you wish to starve." Humor laced his tone.

She ignored him. When she reached the refrigerator, she was delighted to see a bowl of freshly cleaned and boiled shrimp. Had Aminna suspected they'd like something like that for lunch?

"I can make a shrimp salad for lunch, will that work?"

"Fine. I'll be back in twenty minutes. Does that give

you enough time?"

"Sure."

The image of the two of them working intimately together in the kitchen vanished. So much for thinking it a way to get to know her husband better.

Temporary husband!

Their marriage was a business arrangement, nothing more, she admonished herself as she drew plates from the shelves. She didn't want to be here any more than he wanted her here.

She wanted to be out proving herself to her family. To show she could find a niche and make a career.

Sara sighed softly. Photojournalism wasn't it, she admitted to herself. She wasn't exactly sure what was, but there was no use kidding herself. She was washed up as a hotshot reporter—even before she wrote her first big story, too.

Sometimes life wasn't fair.

She loaded a large tray she'd found with the salads, freshly cut home made bread, and glasses of a cola she'd found in the refrigerator. Carrying it carefully, she made her way to the terrace beside the sparkling pool. There was a table conveniently in the shade.

Setting the small table, she was pleased with the way lunch turned out. Now to figure out how to get Kharun out here to eat.

"It looks good."

She jumped at his voice. He'd come up behind her without making a sound.

"Aminna had all the ingredients, so it was easy to throw together."

He seated her and sat opposite. She was pleased to note after the first cautious bite, he dug in with enthusiasm. She tasted the shrimp salad, pleased at how good it was.

Kharun obliquely studied his new bride as they ate. She seemed to pulse with restless energy, looking around her with fresh eyes, smiling in pleasure at the flowers that bloomed near the pool. She seemed to love beauty. He'd noticed that as they'd toured the villa. What other interests did this stranger bound to him have?

"I have work to do this afternoon. At five, however, I plan to go riding. Would you care to join me?" he asked out of the blue. He rarely let others accompany him riding—that was his time for himself. Generally in a hectic week if he could carve out a couple of hours for himself, he guarded the time. Why had he invited Sara to join him?

"I'd love to. Where would we ride?"

"Along the beach. Normally I keep Satin in a stable a few miles from the city. I like to ride in the desert at dusk. But I brought him here a couple of weeks ago. It's not quite the same thing, but a good ride."

"How far can we go before we run into people sunbathing or swimming?"

"If we head away from Staboul, we can go for several miles. In the opposite direction—toward the city, only two. Do you have riding clothes?"

"I have jeans, that'll do for today. Satin's your horse?"

"He is. His Arabian name translates to Satin Magic. There're two other horses at the stables, I'll have one saddled for you. Do you prefer a spirited horse or one who's more sedate?"

"Spirited, of course. I want to ride like the wind along the sea."

Her eyes sparkled when she spoke, the gray going silver with delight. So it wasn't only anger that changed the color. Passion also brought out the silvery lights.

What else did Sara feel passionately about?

He reined in his thoughts. An occasional kiss in public to maintain their charade was one thing. But this woman was a stranger, one who was here under obscure circumstances. There was no passion to be had between them. Once the leases for the oil rights were finalized and signed, they would part ways.

He rose, tossing his napkin on the table. "Lunch was delicious. I'll come for you at five." He turned to walk away before he had second thoughts—on anything.

"Kharun?" She spoke before he reached the door.

"Yes?" He turned. She gathered their plates, stacking them on a tray.

"I wish to go swimming this afternoon. I'll use the pool. I'm sure I'll be okay if there's no one around."

He hesitated, but it was not an option. His young cousin had died when they'd been children—drowned in an accident that had burned deep into his consciousness.

"I'll bring my reading to the terrace while you swim," he said.

"Oh."

She looked nonplused.

He almost smiled. She fascinated him, this Western woman with the changing eyes. "Give me half an hour."

"Sure, I have to clean up and change and all. That's fine. Thanks."

She began humming as she swept the last of the breadcrumbs from the table into her hand, dumping them into one of the used plates.

From jail cell to luxury—Sara seemed to fit into both with a built-in self-sufficiency.

As he headed for his office, he remembered her comment about being uncomfortable at formal gatherings. It was too bad she felt that way. He bet she'd keep people on their toes and intrigue them to boot.

It was forty-five minutes later when Kharun stepped back onto the terrace. He brought his laptop and a stack of folders to skim through. Sara was sitting on the side of the pool, dangling her feet in the water.

For the first time, he was glad he'd worn his sunglasses. He hoped they disguised his reaction to seeing her in that sleek swimsuit. Electric blue, it hugged her body. Her high, firm breasts were clearly displayed, as was her narrow waist and sweet flare of hips. Her legs went on forever when she stood and walked toward the deep end.

"Thanks for coming. I won't swim that long. Then I'll lie in the sun for a while and work on my tan."

He nodded and continued to the table where they'd shared lunch. It remained in the shade and he needed all the cooling he could find. His blood warmed at the sight of her. Desire rose. He enjoyed kissing her—making the best of a bad situation.

Now he wanted her on another level—one that had nothing to do with their bargain or situation.

He wanted her in every way a man wants a woman.

Kharun set his chair so he could watch her without appearing to. She dove neatly into the water and began swimming. Her legs kicked strongly, her arms rose and fell in a steady motion as she cleaved through the water. Turning at the end, she continued to swim. And he continued to watch. She was supple and graceful and strong. Obviously swimming was a sport she enjoyed— and excelled at. It proved a pleasure to watch her.

When at last she rose at the far end and sat on the edge, he looked away. But not before noticing how her breasts rose and fell as she tried to catch her breath. How her wild curls were weighted down with water and hung like shining waves on either side of her face.

And not before he noticed his desire had increased, not diminished. He flipped open the laptop and clicked it on. He had work to do—and it definitely did not include fantasizing about his wife.

His *temporary* wife.

Wife. They were married. Neither were promised to another. And weren't Western women supposed to be much more free with their favors than the women of his culture? Maybe he should explore that.

He looked at Sara. Would she be willing to have an affair while she was here?

Eight

Sara was ready at five for the promised ride. She'd donned sturdy shoes, comfortable jeans, and a sleeveless yellow top. The sun had kissed her skin at the pool, and she had a healthy glow about her.

She'd wondered earlier if Kharun would join her in the pool, but he'd diligently worked all afternoon—never looked up once as far as she could tell.

She'd done some laps, rested on the side, and then swum some more before lying down on a lounge chair at the water's edge.

He'd returned to the house once she'd told him she didn't plan to swim again. In fact, he'd departed so fast she might have been insulted under other circumstances. Would it have hurt to stay a few moments and maybe talk?

She refused to let any vague feeling of disappointment color her excitement for the upcoming ride. She loved horses and often wished she could own one. But with her father's constant travels when she was younger, and her own future uncertain lately, she'd never felt the time was right.

How lucky for Kharun to have a stable close by.

Riding along the beach sounded wildly romantic.

Romantic?

"Fun, I meant fun," she said out loud. "It'll be fun."

A light tap on her door startled her. "Great, now he'll think I talk to myself," she mumbled as she hastened to the door.

"Ready?" Kharun asked. He dressed casually, in light pants and high, glossy riding boots. His loose shirt would shelter him from the sun's rays, yet allow the wind to sweep through keeping him cool in the hot afternoon.

She smiled brightly. "I sure am." And glad to have a respite from being cooped up in the house, but she wouldn't tell him that. She was grateful, actually, for the opportunity to keep her embarrassing mistake from her father.

Obviously not all the servants had taken time off, there were several men working in the stables, which proved to be a short walk from the villa. Two Arabian horses were already saddled, standing in the shade near a water trough.

One was larger than the other, as black as midnight, with a long flowing mane and tail. The second horse was a bay with one white stocking dusting the left rear hoof.

"They're beautiful," Sara said, enchanted. She walked over to them and patted both on the neck. Fumbling in her pocket, she pulled out two carrots which she fed to the well-mannered horses.

"A way to make a friend for life," Kharun said, watching her.

He stood nearby, his feet spread slightly, his hands on his hips. He looked the epitome of a wild desert sheikh. Instead of the lush greenery behind him, he should have had miles of golden desert sand, and the crystal blue of a vast and empty sky. Maybe tents to one side, with his trusty desert raiders with him.

Sara almost shivered in reaction. She was here to ride, not to fantasize.

"This must be Satin Magic," she said, patting the gleaming black horse once more. He was sleek and strong—the perfect mount for Kharun.

"And who's this?" she asked as she ran her hand along the neck of the bay.

"Alia. Don't let her docile air fool you. With a rider on her back, she expects to go places and runs like the wind."

"Sounds great."

"Then, if you are ready?"

Kharun held her waist and boosted her to the horse. Sara could have managed by herself, but kept quiet, savoring the tingling sensations where his hands were. He helped her adjust her stirrups, the brush of his arm and hands against her legs heating her blood more than the sun had.

"All set?" he asked, looking up at her.

"Yes." It came out far more breathless than she'd expected. Turning her horse, she waited for him to mount his.

In only moments they were walking the horses out of the stable yard and down a winding path toward the sea.

The Mediterranean sparkled in the late afternoon sunshine, a deep mysterious blue stretching as far as the eye could see. The brassy glare of the midday sun mellowed as the sun sank lower in the western sky. Colors grew richer. The green of the grass and shrubs gave way to the white of the sand.

Alia seemed impatient, pulling a little on the bit, as if dying to race along the water's edge. Sara wondered if the horse and she were in sync—that's exactly what she yearned to do, too. Race fast enough to escape her thoughts.

As soon as they reached the sand, the horse pranced.

"She's ready to run," Sara said, glancing at Kharun. He looked magnificent. His control of the powerful horse he rode seemed effortless, yet she knew it was a demonstration of his skill. Horse and rider looked perfect together.

"Then let's oblige her," he said with a sudden wicked grin. Without a visible sign, he gave his horse his head and Satin Magic stretched out into a controlled canter, sand kicking up behind him.

"We can't let them get ahead of us," Sara said as she urged Alia into a gallop, her own competitive instincts rising.

In seconds both horses were running neck and neck along the pristine beach, sand spraying behind the thundering hoofs. The breeze from the Mediterranean enhanced the feeling of speed as they let their horses set the pace.

Sara laughed out loud, feeling wild and free. It was exhilarating! She felt as if she could ride forever. As if only the darkness of night could slow them down and maybe not even then. Alia was a magical horse with a smooth gait and easy disposition. Sara was falling in love with her after only a few minutes. Could they ride every day?

The beach stretched out ahead of them, the blue of the water a blur to the right as the horses seemed to gallop for pure joy. Stretching their legs, bunching and shifting muscles, gaits smooth and synchronous, as if they'd matched strides a million times in the past and would many times again.

Several minutes later Kharun slowed from a gallop to an easy canter. Sara followed suit. It was almost as exciting as a flat-out, go-for-broke run and easier on the horses. She watched where they were going, but took time to enjoy the remoteness of the beach, the cool breeze from the water, the splashes when an errant finger of water crossed their path and they plunged through.

Finally, in the distance, she saw signs of others on the beach. Kharun motioned for her to slow down. She complied instantly, bringing Alia to a complete stop. Both she and her horse were breathing hard. Her blood pumped through her veins. She felt exhilarated.

"That was fabulous!" she said when Kharun reined in beside her. "That's the public beach ahead, I take it?"

"Yes. We can continue for another half mile if you like, but at a much slower pace. I do not wish to take the horses where people are using the beach."

"Let's go as far as we can, then."

She walked her horse and Kharun came along beside her, his knee almost brushing against hers. She could have reached out to touch him with no effort. She glanced his way.

His hair was tousled from their run, but he didn't appear to be having trouble catching his breath. He slid a look in her direction.

"You ride well," he said.

"I told you, the best lessons money could buy. I always wanted a horse, but talk about impractical with Dad's job and all."

"If you like, I can arrange for you to ride while you are here. As long as you're accompanied by a groom," Kharun said.

"You're not very trusting. Do you think I'll up and ride away never to return?"

He shrugged. "It wouldn't matter if you tried, I would come after you."

His words sent a shiver down her back. He would. They had an agreement. But even beyond that—her leaving would humiliate him beyond anything. That would prove an even worse situation than the incident caused by being caught taking illegal photographs.

"I wouldn't do that," she said.

"You would do nothing to jeopardize your father's career, right?" His voice held a mocking tone.

Sara flared up. "That's true. But that's not the only reason. I gave you my word and that means something to me. As long as the situation is as it is, you have nothing to worry about with me, Kharun. I stand by my promises. I said I'd stay until everyone signs the stupid leases and I will. I said I'd pretend this was a great marriage and I will. I've done nothing to give you cause to think otherwise."

"It's still early days. Who knows what you might do given the opportunity."

She could tell from his tone he was skeptical. She chafed at the restrictions but reminded herself she'd brought it all on due to her impetuous actions. Time would show him he could trust her.

None of that mattered right now. The ride wasn't over. She'd enjoy each moment as it came.

So she could remember after she returned home?

The thought surprised her. Would she want memories about her mock marriage? It was a sham entered into solely to prevent a scandal.

She began to wonder what a real marriage to Kharun would be like.

Would he follow his father's example and marry for passionate love? Or would he follow the dictates of his aunt and marry for dynastic reasons?

Her own parents had a solid, loving marriage. Yet she didn't want a marriage like her mother's. Sara wanted to be a person in her own right; have her own interests and goals. Her own career. Not put her husband's ahead of her own all the time.

Her mother was the perfect businessman's wife, loved to host parties, mingle with strangers, wear the right gown and always knew what to do at the right time. She always knew the right thing to say.

As Kharun's wife would need to.

Sara sighed. It'd be hard to follow in such a paragon's steps.

"Why the sigh?" Kharun asked.

"What? Oh, I was thinking about my mother."

"She's a lovely woman. You will look as lovely when you're her age," he said.

She looked at him in startled surprise. "I will?"

He nodded once, abruptly.

"Thank you. That's one of the nicest compliments I've ever had."

Made even more special coming from a man who didn't appear to like her, or trust her.

"But Mom's a hard act to follow. She always knows what to say, what to wear, how to act."

"Perhaps that's her calling in life. She's made a niche for herself as your father's supporter. Somehow, I don't see you in a similar role."

Sara grinned at him. "Got it in one!"

"So what do you want to do in life, Sara Kinsale?"

Her grin faded. "I don't have a clue. That's what makes it so hard. My sister Margaret knew she wanted to be an attorney from the day she started high school. Josh was scientific-minded from kindergarten, so they tell me. I know my parents despair of me ever settling down."

She didn't want to mention how pleased her mother had been that she married Kharun. Like that was a career choice.

She had to find something she was good at and liked so she could pursue it. She'd hoped the photojournalist job would be it. She'd been taking pictures since she was little and had a flair for it. But she'd blown her first major assignment.

"Did you always know you would one day run your family's business?" she asked.

He shook his head. "When I was growing up, I

wanted to drive race cars, fly airplanes and pilot a submarine. But as I grew older, business fascinated me. Especially after my father let me work in various departments of the different family companies between school terms. I was hooked."

She was delighted to learn this tidbit about the serious man beside her. Who would have thought he once had frivolous ideas?

"So did you pursue any of those subjects in school? Maybe not piloting a submarine, but maybe racing?"

"Flying. I have a multi-engine license. But never achieved the others. By the time I was sent away to school, my father made it clear business acumen was important. So I focused my studies in that direction. My family has several interests that span shipping, manufacturing and exporting. That was the role I trained for."

"Did you want it?" she asked.

Dynastic family responsibilities were beyond her experience. She couldn't ever dream of doing what her father did, much less go into a line of work she might not like.

"I find it much more challenging and rewarding than trying to get the consensus of a bunch of ministers each of whom seem to have their own agenda rather than the good of the country."

"I can see why."

"My father loved that challenge. He'd often talk about it at dinner."

"Do you have to run the companies now? Can't you go back to your earlier dreams?"

"One cannot fight one's destiny. Surely you know that by now," he said.

Was it her destiny to roam restlessly searching forever for some career that would hold meaning and interest?

Kharun drew up his horse. "Here's the path back to the stable. Have you had enough riding for today?"

"Yes. It's been great. But it's been such a long time since I've been riding my legs are a bit stiff already."

He led the way along the path until the stable came into view. Dismounting when the grooms ran out, Kharun tossed the reins to one.

Sara slid off her horse before Kharun could come around to help her and smiled at the groom who took the reins.

"Whoa," she said, as she took a step and felt her legs fold up beneath her. Before she could hit the ground, however, Kharun's arms were around her, beneath her knees, behind her back. In one swoop he picked her up and held her against his chest.

"I can walk," she protested, leaning a little into his masculine strength. Of course she could walk, but what woman in the world never fantasized about some dashing, romantic man sweeping her off her feet and into his arms?

"Your legs will feel wobbly for a while. Sit and rest." He set her on a bench near the side of the stable.

Sara blinked. She had visions of Kharun carrying her through the flower-scented garden, through the opened French doors to her bedroom and —

Get a grip, she told herself, feeling the heat of

embarrassment sweep up her cheeks.

"You're right, I'll be fine in a minute."

She couldn't look at him. What if he suspected where her wild thoughts were running? Theirs was a contrived marriage, lasting only as long as the negotiations continued. There were no romantic overtones, no enduring emotions between them.

But for a moment, Sara didn't think there had to be. They were married. He'd kissed her a couple of times already. She looked up at him, her eyes focused on his mouth. She wanted more from him. And she suspected he wouldn't turn her down. What would happen if she kissed him?

Nine

Kharun sat at his desk in the study the next morning when Piers knocked on the open door and stuck his head in.

"Got a moment?" he asked. "I took a chance and came by early to bring you the latest changes."

"Come in. I wondered if you'd drop by this morning or we'd meet at the office." Kharun put down the report he was reading and motioned his longtime friend and most trusted adviser to enter.

"Honeymoon over?" Piers asked, grinning at his friend. He carried his briefcase over to the desk and placed it in a cleared area, then sat in his usual spot.

"Such as it was."

"And?"

"Not that it's any of your business, but it's more difficult being married than I'd anticipated."

"An engagement would have been better."

"But probably would not have fooled Garah, Hamin and the others."

Piers laughed. "A hastily planned ceremony doesn't make a marriage."

"It's binding enough."

"True, but an annulment will be easy once the negotiations finish."

He opened his briefcase and pulled out a folder. "The latest from Samuel Kinsale. Do you think he's mellowing because his daughter married you? It seems we may close the deal sooner than expected."

Kharun looked up at that. "I can't imagine that tough businessman softening for anyone. How soon?"

Piers shrugged. "Within a few days it looks like. Going to New York for the signing?"

"That's where his corporate offices are. I thought I'd take a trip there when time to sign. Now, I'm not so sure."

"I might join you if you go. How about your wife?"

"Sara will be thrilled to hear the negotiations are progressing so well. She originally came to be with her parents while they're here. I suspect she'll wish to continue that vacation when we separate. Has there been any further repercussions due to her actions?"

"All's quiet on the Garah and Hamin front. I think they are beginning to cave on their stance. It wouldn't look good, challenging the new wife of the country's negotiator, now would it?"

"And when we separate?" Kharun leaned back in his chair and studied his adviser. "What will be the repercussions then?"

"Ah, good question. Perhaps they'll surge back stronger than ever in their anti-progress stance. Who can say at this point?"

Kharun rose and walked to the open doors. He didn't notice the beautiful blossoms in full bloom. Nor the glimpse of the sea beyond. He saw instead Sara's laughing face when she was happy, the sparkle in her silvery eyes when she was angry, and the graceful feminine way she had of walking or swimming or riding.

"Something wrong?" Piers asked, watching Kharun curiously.

"What would be the ramifications of a divorce instead of an annulment?" Kharun asked without turning.

The silence stretched out behind him.

Finally he turned to meet Piers's puzzled gaze.

"I don't understand." He blinked, slapped the side of his forehead with the heel of his hand. "Oh, damn, I do understand. Kharun, you and she didn't—"

"It's a hypothetical question," Kharun said firmly.

At least at this point. But the desire he felt around Sara seemed to escalate each time he saw her. And he knew she was aware of the sparks that seemed to fly between them.

Yesterday at the stables, for a moment, he'd thought she'd start something. She'd looked at him intently, then color had risen in her cheeks. She'd been distant ever since.

What had she been thinking?

Piers cleared his throat. "Actually, it might be better to divorce, than have an annulment. More believable, if you know what I mean."

"Elaborate."

"Let's face it, Kharun, no one in their right mind will think you and she did nothing—unless the marriage was a sham. It's one thing to fool your ministers—something else to let them know they've been fooled."

"Ah, so now you think it expedient to get a divorce rather than an annulment?"

"Can I have a few days to think over the situation?" Piers asked warily.

"Take as long as you like. It's hypothetical."

"But for how long, I wonder," his friend asked.

Sara appeared in the doorway, stopping suddenly when she saw Piers.

"Oh, excuse me, I didn't know you had company."

"Come in, Sara. You remember Piers."

"The best man. How are you?" She smiled warily, but remained at the doorway.

"Was there something you wanted?" Kharun asked politely.

"I wanted to call my mother. She'll wonder why I haven't contacted her at all. I mean, I came here to visit them, then disappeared. The next thing she knew, she was attending my wedding."

"She knows you are here and safe," Kharun said.

"So I can't call her?"

"You may." He gestured to the phone on the desk.

Piers rose, but Kharun shook his head.

He turned to Kharun. "Is that wise?"

"Is it wise to raise her parent's suspicions by not allowing her contact?"

She remained in the doorway, watching the interchange. "I can wait until later, when you've finished your business," she said turning to leave.

"This gets more complicated by the moment," Piers said.

"It'd be all right to let her call whenever she wishes. Sara gave me her word she'd abide by the terms of our agreement. I trust her to do that."

Piers blinked at that comment. "You? Trust a woman?"

"Within limits."

"That's a first. I thought after Andrea du Polline you'd sworn never to trust a woman again."

"This situation's different. Sara worries about her father's reputation, as well."

"As well as her own desire to stay out of one of our jails," Piers muttered sarcastically.

"That can be a strong motivating factor," Kharun agreed. "What did Kinsale concede on?"

Piers opened the folder he'd brought and looked at his friend. "I trust you know what you're doing about your marriage. And about the leases. Tell me what you think about this new counteroffer?"

He indicated the paragraph of the report.

Kharun knew Piers was surprised by his comment. Hadn't he said often enough in the past he didn't trust women? They all appeared to be after one thing—his money. From his younger days in Saint Albans, to his college days, and even the beginnings of his career, beautiful women professed an interest—but had an eye on his inheritance.

Twice he'd come close to asking a woman to marry him, only to discover before he could ask that they were more interested in his wealth than their relationship. More interested in being seen in all the right places than in quiet dinners away from the clubs.

How ironic, now he married a woman who didn't even *profess* to care for him.

But by the same token, neither did she seem especially interested in his wealth or indulging in hectic nightlife.

Sara wandered around the patio feeling frustrated and bored. She needed to talk to her mother—though she'd have to reassure her she was deliriously happy. And then run the risk of making plans for a dinner together in the not-too-distant future.

Her mother was big on family. She'd adopt Kharun into their extended family immediately.

Plopping down on a chaise longue, Sara moodily contemplated the situation between Kharun and her mother. How would he take to her family's informal gatherings? Was he too steeped in tradition to fit in easily with a more casual private life? What did it matter? Theirs was a temporary alliance. They could stall any family overtures until time to separate.

For some reason, the thought didn't make her happy.

"Bonjour, Sara." Kharun's mother stood in the doorway and smiled at her.

Sara scrambled to her feet surprised to see Angelique. Did Kharun know his mother was here?

"Good morning. I didn't know you were coming. Would you like to sit here or is it too warm? Perhaps you'd rather go inside," she replied smiling warmly at the woman.

"Here, of course," Angelique said as she strolled onto the terrace. "The roses are particularly beautiful this year. But Matassin's a master gardener and has a special affinity for roses." She sat on the chair beside Sara's and indicated Sara should resume her own seat.

"I understand Kharun's back at work. So tiresome. I know there's a lot to do, but I do hope it won't be long before he can delegate to others enough to allow time off—if he ever does. His father loved his work. Runs in the family, I guess. I understand he's planning to go to the states to celebrate when the oil leases are signed. Maybe you and he can squeeze out a few extra days for a honeymoon then. You could show him your home—though I'm sure he's already seen it."

Sara smiled politely. It was the first she'd heard about a possible trip back to the States. That could simplify things when they separated. She'd have to speak to Kharun about the trip.

"I came suspecting he was back at work. I know my son, you see," Angelique said.

"Piers was here first thing this morning to see him."

"Then perhaps while they attend to business you'd like to have lunch with me and Jasmine. Then you and I could stop in a few boutiques afterward, to look for a dress for Friday. Unless you already have a gown you planned to wear."

"Friday?" Sara asked.

"The reception at the British embassy. I'm sure Kharun plans to attend. He wouldn't risk slighting anyone by not attending."

"Friday night?" What were the chances their sham marriage would be over by then? Probably slim to none.

Drat, she hated formal receptions. Especially any in which she was sure to be the center of attention. And as the new bride of Kharun bak Rijad, she knew she'd be at the top of the list of people to stare at and gossip about.

"I wasn't sure if you brought an appropriate dress, but I'd be delighted to introduce you to the delights of several boutiques in Staboul which can provide the most fabulous gowns on short notice."

Sara wondered if one of them was the place Jasmine had found her wedding gown only an hour before the wedding.

"I would appreciate that. I don't have anything suitable for an embassy reception. And, I'd love to come to lunch." Anything would be preferable to her almost enforced stay at the villa.

Angelique knew nothing of the truth. Jasmine knew and didn't trust her. It should prove to be an interesting lunch.

Aminna appeared in the doorway, Sara's camera in hand.

"I found this in the kitchen when I returned this morning." Aminna held it out.

"My camera." Sara rose and crossed to the doorway to take it. "I left it there yesterday when I fixed lunch." Automatically, Sara checked the camera indicator.

"There's a memory card in it."

Aminna nodded gravely. "I saw it was empty and got a replacement. Do you wish to have lunch in the dining room or on the terrace?"

"I'm taking my new daughter-in-law out to lunch, Aminna. Please inform Kharun."

Aminna nodded gravely and left.

"What a complicated camera. I didn't know you

were a photographer. How exciting. What do you like to shoot?" Angelique asked.

Pictures of your summer home without your knowledge, popped into Sara's mind.

"Um, I'm still developing my style. I like working to get the right framing, contrast the light and shadows. Things like that."

"What do you photograph? People? Scenes?"

"Horses, odd houses, old ruins." She smiled. "Sometimes people. Whatever I find interesting."

She'd been taking photographs of her family and friends since she'd been a child. When traveling with her parents, she took pictures of exotic locations. The results were gratifying.

She'd been focused on her aborted plan to get pictures of the Rijad's summer place, hoping for unusual angles to make the shots distinctive. Maybe today she could take snapshots of Staboul to take home when she left.

And later, she'd photograph the villa. Surely no one could find fault with her taking photos of her own home, however temporary.

Aminna came quietly onto the terrace, a laden tray of tea and small cakes in her hands. She efficiently set the table, placed the food in the center and returned to the house, never saying a word.

"I'd love to photograph her," Sara said musingly. "Her face has such character."

She faced Angelique as she poured their tea. "And I'd love to photograph your son riding Satin Magic."

"Do so. If it turns out, I would love to have a copy.

He's a fine-looking man, isn't he?" She looked at Sara from beneath her lashes.

The true reason his mother had come—to find out more about her son's new wife.

Sara smiled politely, wondering how his mother would feel if she knew Sara's true feelings.

Suddenly, she realized she wasn't even sure of her true feelings. She felt confined to the house since he'd rescued her from the jail. Understandable, though frustrating. She was counting the days until she would be free.

Yet she was strangely intrigued by the man. Fascinated by the range of sensations that danced through her when in his presence. She liked sparring with him, liked hearing him discuss the matters of change he wanted for his country.

She was completely captivated by his kisses. She warmed at the memory. The last time they'd had someone not privy to their secret come to visit, he'd kissed her. Would he kiss her in his mother's presence?

Her heart rate sped up a notch.

She'd soon find out. Kharun stepped out onto the terrace.

Ten

"Ma Mere, Aminna told me you were here. I wasn't expecting you." Kharun glanced at Sara as he crossed the terrace to kiss his mother on both cheeks.

"I didn't mean to interrupt you, *chéri*. Aminna told me you were hard at work. I thought Sara might have enticed you away from your duties for a little longer. First you take no honeymoon, now you neglect her. For shame." The twinkle in her eyes belied her words.

"Things needed to be done. Sara understands," he replied, pulling out a chair and sitting at the small table.

"Always things need to be done. Your new wife's a saint if she allows it. Such virtue deserves a reward. I'm taking Sara to lunch with me and Jasmine. Unless you have plans yourself."

"Piers is here. We'll be busy a little longer."

"Times have changed from when I was young," she said mockingly, with a conspiratorial look at Sara.

"How so?"

"Your father and I made sure our priorities included a long honeymoon."

"It never ended."

Her face saddened. "Not until his death. Cherish the moments you have, *chéri*, they seem so fleeting in retrospect."

She rose and patted him on the cheek. "I will speak with Aminna for a moment, then Sara and I will leave. We're going shopping after lunch. Bring your camera, Sara, you can start with Jasmine and me."

He waited until she was out of hearing, then turned to Sara, apparently noticing the camera for the first time.

"Aminna brought me the camera. She found it in the kitchen," Sara said, holding it in front of her, almost like a shield. "Your mother suggested the photographs."

"Take all the pictures she wants, then. But I'll have final say on how you use the pictures," he said with a warning in his tone. "And none are to go to your newspaper!"

Sara stiffened. She knew he didn't trust her, totally due to her own actions, but it still rankled. "I have no intention of sending any to the paper!"

"Jasmine knows the true story about our marriage, but my mother doesn't. Keep it that way," he admonished.

"Did you come out here to tell me that? I can remember that order from one day to the next. No one is to know. If I can't tell my mother, I surely won't be telling yours!"

She rose and hurried into the house to change from the modest white pants she'd donned that morning into something more suitable to lunch with her new in-laws.

When she entered the large foyer several minutes later, Piers and Angelique were talking. Kharun leaned casually against the priceless Louis XV table watching them. He looked at Sara when she joined them. She wondered for a moment if the gleam in his eyes meant more than he still didn't trust her.

"Have a good afternoon," he said, deliberately crossing over to her. He stood so close she could almost share his breath—if she hadn't been holding hers.

"I wish I were going with you," he whispered. Only she understood the full truth of the comment. He was wary about letting her out of his sight. Yet his comment undoubtedly sounded totally different to his mother. She was sure. Angelique thought Kharun longed to spend the day with his new bride.

If she only knew!

"I'll be back this afternoon—nothing will happen." It was the best she could do to offer reassurance.

His lips brushed against hers and he straightened and turned.

It wasn't enough. Sara gripped the straps of her purse tightly. She wanted more!

Yet the brief kiss was only Kharun's way to keep up the charade.

Pasting a bright smile on her face she faced Angelique. "Let's do lunch!"

When the women left, Piers looked at Kharun. "Is that wise? Letting Sara go out with your mother? Angelique has a way of inviting confidences."

"Maybe not the wisest thing I could do. But if I'd keep Sara isolated from my mother, she'd wonder why she couldn't get to know her new daughter-in-law better and question me—and speculate to all and sundry. I don't want to raise any suspicions."

"I understand, but what's to stop Sara from running off the first moment Angelique turns her back?"

Kharun paused a moment, deep in thought. "Sara said she would stay, I believe her."

"She could be a spy. At best she's a sensationalist hack journalist searching for fodder for that rag she works for."

"But she *is* Samuel Kinsale's daughter. His ethics have never been questioned. I'm betting she's enough like her father that she won't disappear."

"I hope you're right," Piers said, heading back toward the office.

"Me, too," Kharun said softly. He wasn't sure where the feeling of trust had come from. His experience with women outside his family had done nothing to foster such a trust. And he really didn't know her well enough to know how she would react once away from the villa.

But there was something about Sara—

He shook his head and followed his friend back to the office. He hoped he wasn't letting his desire for the woman cloud his judgment.

When Angelique's chauffeur dropped Sara back at the villa later that afternoon, Sara held a half dozen bags of purchases gripped in both hands. She rang the bell and wondered if she should have asked for a key.

One maid opened the door, smiling shyly when she recognized Sara. She said something in Arabic, which Sara didn't understand. Replying in French, she could tell the young woman didn't speak that language. It was frustrating not being able to communicate. But the nods and smiles seemed sufficient.

Sara headed for her room. The afternoon had been unexpectedly fun. Jasmine never let up her cautious air, which thankfully Angelique didn't appear to notice. Sara answered all their questions, dared to ask a couple of her own, and tried to pretend everything was normal for a newly wed woman getting to know her new in-laws.

But she never let herself forget the situation with Kharun and the reality of their relationship.

"Shopping, a woman's delight," Kharun said behind her.

Sara spun around, the packages swinging.

"I didn't hear you!" she said. How did he move so soundlessly?

"Did you enjoy your afternoon?"

"Very much. Your mother's a delight. And given time, I might even come to like your sister. But she wasn't as openly friendly as your mother."

"Because she knows of the charade. My mother suspected nothing?"

"If you mean our marriage, she's a romantic, I'd say. She thinks this is a fairy-tale romance and is so happy her little boy found the right woman."

Kharun looked taken aback for a second.

Sara smiled and turned and continued to her bedroom.

Kharun followed her into the bedroom as if he had every right. Which, she thought wryly, he did.

"I bought a few things," she said needlessly, dumping her bags on the bed. Kharun glanced at the bags and the labels from the boutiques. He then looked at her, his dark eyes mesmerizing. She fidgeted beneath his gaze.

"What did you buy?" he asked politely.

"A dress for the reception at the British embassy. Your mother said we'd be going. And I figured I couldn't wear safari outfits, or sun dresses."

He nodded his head once.

"When were you planning on telling me about the reception?" she asked. "Ten minutes before we were about to leave? What if I hadn't bought something suitable? Listen Kharun, arranging my life without telling me isn't something I'm willing to put up with." She waved her hands. "The first I knew about our wedding was when Jasmine showed up with the dress. The first I knew about this reception was when your mother told me. What else's going on that I need to know that you haven't told me?"

He shrugged. "I'll have to check my calendar. Would you like to go over it with me?" he asked, amusement dancing in his eyes.

She flushed at the sardonic glint in his eyes. She tilted her chin.

"Sounds like a plan especially if you have something penciled in you expect me to attend. And I will let you know."

He quirked an eyebrow. "An event you and I would attend that you arranged?"

"My mother'll certainly wish to have us over for dinner soon. The few moments we had to talk after our hasty wedding weren't enough to satisfy her curiosity. Nor could we talk while I packed with you hovering around like a vulture."

"Vulture? Somehow I'd hoped for a more romantic turn of phrase. I thought I played the part of doting bridegroom perfectly."

"I'm sure you'd have received rave reviews if anyone had known. But my mother's big on family. She'll love welcoming you into ours, the sooner the better for her."

Sara bit her lower lip. "We'll have to stall her."

"Why?"

"There's no point in her getting used to you when the marriage will be over soon."

He studied her a moment longer, then looked at the bags on the bed.

"Let me see the dress you bought."

He hadn't responded to her statement. She thought about pressing the issue, but about what? She knew this was solely a marriage of convenience—his convenience. She'd do her best to keep him away from her mother and hope the leases were signed soon enough for her to get out unscathed.

Showing him the clothes changed the subject. Sara loved her selections and wondered what he'd think. She pushed aside two of the smaller bags, taking the larger one. Withdrawing the dress, wrapped in layers and layers of tissue paper, she shook it free.

Almost a midnight-blue, shot through with silver threads, it was the loveliest dress she'd ever seen. And it fit like a dream.

She held it up and looked at him.

His expression gave nothing away.

"Try it on," he invited.

"Now?"

"It's hard to see how it will look on you when merely held up in front." He walked to the sitting area and sat as if he planned to stay the rest of the afternoon.

She sighed and went into the bathroom.

Five minutes later Sara emerged wearing the new dress.

The jeweled halter neckline gave a false impression of modesty belied by the fitted bodice and the long slinky skirt that sported a slit up one side to mid-thigh. The back was virtually nonexistent until her waist. Sara felt alluring and mysterious wearing it.

She should have found the shoes first, however. Walking barefoot did not complete the look she was going for.

Maybe it didn't matter—not if the heightened awareness of Kharun's interest was a gauge.

He rose and walked to meet her halfway across the room.

"You look exquisite," he said slowly, his gaze running along the length of her body. Heat built as he continued to study her. "Turn around."

Slowly she turned around completely, hearing the hiss as he drew in a sharp breath when he saw her bare back.

"Won't you be cold in that?" he asked, his voice rough.

Sara shook her head. In fact, if she didn't bank the fires his look caused, she'd burn up.

"I think I'll be fine," she said, pleased to hear her own voice sounded normal. "Your mother helped pick it out."

"My mother's a French woman, of course she'd pick out something wildly sexy."

"Wildly sexy? Cool!" She smiled involuntarily. No one had ever said that about her before.

He reached out to draw a warm finger down her bare arm. "The men will be envious of my good fortune. The women will be jealous of your beauty," he said slowly.

Her heart almost flipped over. No doubt about it, this man she'd married was a charmer. No one had ever said anything so wonderful to her before.

Mesmerized by the heat in his eyes, Sara stared back at him, licking suddenly dry lips.

Kharun caught the movement and fastened his attention on her mouth.

Before she could say anything, he drew her into his arms and kissed her.

There was no audience, was her last coherent thought before dazzling sensation took over.

Eleven

His mouth sparked a cascade of shimmering enchantment. Sara stepped closer, as if seeking more. She parted her lips and instantly felt Kharun deepen the kiss. His warm hands on her bare back sent tingling waves of excitement coursing through her. His tongue dancing with hers caused the desire that simmered to explode.

She yearned for more. She couldn't get enough of him. She wanted to taste him everywhere, touch him everywhere. Her hands threaded through his thick hair, relishing the texture and heat. She moved them to trace the muscles of his shoulders, back to his head. When he slowly spun them around, she felt as if the world tilted. She clung, holding on to the one steadfast reality in a fantasy illusion.

Slowly they moved until she felt the world fall away. The two of them fell onto the bed, amid the bags, tissue paper and pillows.

He held her tightly, cushioning their soft fall, moving his mouth from hers to her cheek, tracing her jaw, running his tongue lightly against her throat, kissing that frantically beating pulse point.

Sara lay half across him, feeling the rugged strength of his chest beneath her. Savoring the feel of his hands against her skin, touching her, caressing her.

The fresh breeze blowing across the garden from the sea brought with it the scent of flowers and the salt air but no cooling relief for the building heat. She relished the sensations that clamored for dominance—desire, enchantment, sensuous languor.

When Kharun ran his hand down her side, slipping beneath the bodice of the gown to graze her breast, Sara caught her breath. For an instant sanity reasserted itself.

She pushed back, gazing down at him. Slowly he opened his eyes and gazed back.

Scrambling off the bed, Sara backed away. The breeze suddenly felt cold. The dress offered so little protection.

"What's going on?" she asked. The forceful demand she'd hoped to make came out almost a whisper.

Kharun rose lithely and took a step toward her. Sara backed away, clinging almost desperately to the shred of common sense that told her things were getting out of hand. One part of her wanted to throw herself back into his embrace. Another part questioned her sanity.

"I kissed you, you kissed me back."

"That went far beyond a mere kiss!"

"And that upsets you?"

"Of course it does. We agreed to a farce of a marriage to make sure we avoided a scandal. But we agreed it would be strictly platonic."

"I'm afraid I don't remember such an agreement," he said, his eyes narrowed as he gazed into hers.

She blinked. They'd said—what exactly? "I remember in the car—"

He waited, silently, without moving, but aware of everything.

Sara took a nervous step backward.

Her eyes widened as she remembered. They'd been discussing the right to share a bed. She'd said he had to stay out of hers and she'd stay out of his. But now that she recalled the conversation, he'd never agreed.

"The dress was a mistake," she said.

"Why? It looks lovely on you."

"It sends the wrong message."

Kharun laughed and shook his head, heading for the door.

"Sara, the sight of you in that dress doesn't inflame passion."

He paused at the door and looked back at her. "Just looking at you does that. Whether in jeans or bedraggled khakis. I came to see if you wished to ride again this afternoon?"

She blinked, trying to regain her balance.

Had he said he felt desire for her every time he looked at her?

Then he asked about riding?

"Ride?"

"Horses?"

The sardonic glint was back. He probably thought her mind had been short circuited by their kiss.

He wasn't far off the mark.

"Yes, I'd love to go riding. I'll change and meet you at the stables."

Kharun waited impatiently in the foyer for Sara to change. He didn't trust himself to stay in her room while she slipped out of that sexy gown and donned jeans.

He hadn't wanted to stop when she'd called a halt. He wanted her. And it'd been a long time since he'd felt such a strong sense of wanting for a woman.

Brief flings in distant capitals had been the norm over the last few years after his blazing mistake with Andrea du Polline. He'd made a fool of himself over her. She'd made a fool of herself over his money.

And since his father's death, he hadn't had the time, nor inclination, to seek female companionship.

Sara was different. Was that part of the spark that drove him crazy? He was sure she felt something around him. He was too savvy not to recognize the signs. Their kiss had been all he'd hoped. Too bad she'd stopped long before he was ready.

He almost laughed. She thought it was the dress. Did she really not have a clue? Or was she playing a more devious game?

"I'm ready."

Sara joined him, dressed in jeans, a long-sleeved cotton top and her shoes. He'd have to see about her getting some riding boots. Especially if they went to the desert. Would Sara like riding across the dunes chasing the stars at night?

They could escape away from everything—until they were alone in the universe. He'd dismount and help her from the saddle, letting her body slide down his, a temptation he knew he couldn't resist. Spreading a blanket on the sands still warm from the day's sun, he'd lay her down and strip her bare—until her soft, feminine skin was bathed in starlight. Then he'd make love to her until dawn.

"Kharun, are we going?"

He looked at her. Yes, one night he'd take her to the desert and make love to her.

"After you." He opened the door and waited.

She preceded him and turned toward the walkway that led to the stables. He watched her walk, tall and proud. Her hips swayed gently in the tight jeans.

He felt his own pants tighten against him. But he couldn't look away. He thought about what Piers had said—better a divorce than an annulment—at least the ministers might be fooled by such a decision. An annulment would be a slap in the face.

After everyone had met her, no one'd believe an annulment anyway.

Theirs was a temporary alliance, true. But Kharun knew something bound them tightly for however long she stayed. He'd make Sara his wife in truth as well as on paper.

When they reached the stables, he reached out and took an arm, halting her.

"What?"

"To make sure you know, it wasn't the dress."

He leaned over to kiss her again, pleased to note the instant response on her part.

The horses were already saddled. Kharun helped Sara to mount, then swung up onto his own. He led the way to the beach, wishing again he was on the desert. The confines of the city and demands of his new position grated. He needed to feel the space and freedom of the desert. Soon, he'd schedule a week and forget Staboul and his uncle's interfering ministers and show Sara the other delights of his country.

Once he reached the beach, he gave Satin Magic his head. He wasn't surprised to find Sara racing neck and neck beside him in only seconds. Alia was a match for Satin. He urged his horse to greater speed, relishing the sense of freedom, the exhilaration riding Satin always brought.

They thundered down the beach, splashing in the shallows, scattering rainbows of colors behind them, tossing up the sand in a wake they could track. Purely for his own pleasure, Kharun kept up the fast pace, but he also kept a close watch on Sara. If it became too much, he'd stop.

She was a woman to rise to challenges. She did her best to coax a faster gait from Alia, never giving up.

The sun sparkled on the water, the air scented with the fragrance of a thousand flowers. Blood pulsed in his veins. It was a great day in which to be alive--made all the more so with Sara's presence.

The thought caught him by surprise.

Seeing the people ahead on the beach, he slowed Satin. Alia raced past, then slowed and turned. Sara halted, breathing hard, as she waited for Kharun to reach her. Her face was ablaze with happiness.

"That was wonderful!" she said, then burst into laughter. "What a fantasy—racing a sheikh along the sea. Splashing in the water. I'm wet to my knees."

He felt a chill. Was that all the afternoon meant—a

fantasy with a title, instead of the real thing with a man who desired her? Was she like the others, caught up in the trappings of wealth and titles?

Even after the hard run, Alia danced in place, eager to continue.

"What's wrong?" Sara asked, controlling her mount.

"Not a thing. You ride well." He'd better keep reality in mind.

"It's easy on a sweetie like Alia. She seems ready to continue."

"They have a lot of stamina. I breed them for endurance," he said.

"Do you ever take them out in the desert?"

Had her mind aligned itself with his? Was it fate?

"Sometimes."

"I'd love to try that, if we get a chance. I imagine it's even more wonderful—riding forever in the empty desert. No sign of civilization for miles and miles. There are places like that in the States and I love being there. Maybe I should have been a hermit in another life."

He edged his horse closer, facing Sara, until their knees almost touched.

She was still breathing fast, her breasts rising and falling rapidly. Her gaze caught his, drifted to his mouth. Did she want another kiss? Was she as caught up in the sensual awareness as he?

Her lids drooped and she looked away, color staining her cheeks.

Kharun felt a wave of satisfaction sweep through. She couldn't hide her own interest. He hoped it was only a matter of time before he had her in his bed.

Knowing that possibility existed gave him the will to be patient. He wouldn't rush her.

Sara started her horse back toward the villa. Kharun turned and eased Satin Magic into step with Alia. The horses tossed their heads, but he and Sara kept them to a walk.

"What else was in the packages you brought home?" he asked.

"Another dress and a couple of pairs of shoes. Your mother's a power shopper. She was telling us at lunch how she splurges every now and then to go to Paris, where 'they know how to dress a woman'."

"For her, that's the only place worth shopping."

"Yet she loves this country, that much is evident in her conversation." Sara cast a sidelong glance. "And she's very proud of you."

"And you find that surprising? Aren't most mothers for their children?"

"Does she know the real you?"

"Who is the real me?"

"A man who manipulates events to his own purposes."

Kharun suspected where the conversation headed. Could he defuse it?

"Did you take pictures?"

"I got some great ones. Jasmine was quite annoyed with me by the end of the afternoon. Every time I'd see something new, I'd ask Yasaf, your mother's chauffeur, to stop. Your mother, on the other hand, seemed happy to have me photograph anything that took my fancy—from the lovely inlays lining the outside of a mosque, to the faces of children in the poorer section of town."

"You went to the Sadinn area of town?"

"I think that's what it was called. Angelique gave me a complete tour before we stopped at the first boutique."

Why had his mother done so? She didn't know the full circumstances of his marriage, but even if it'd been a true love match, wouldn't she shelter her new daughter-in-law from the rougher sections of town until Sara became more accustomed to their country?

"Your mother kept the camera so she can look at the pictures. I'm sure she can assure you I'm not photographing top secret places in my role as spy."

Twelve

Kharun was going to drive her crazy, Sara knew it. It wasn't enough he suspected her of being a spy, now he was on some campaign to seduce her. Did he think she'd confess to some nefarious plot?

She paused with mascara wand in hand and peered into the mirror. Ten more minutes before they were due to depart for the British embassy reception.

Sara glanced over to the bed and looked at the dress. Would she ever be able to wear it without remembering Kharun's kisses and caresses the afternoon she modeled it for him?

She doubted it. She looked back to the mirror and touched her lashes with the mascara. She was nervous about the evening. She disliked large gatherings, how would she ever handle being the mysterious new bride of Sheikh Kharun bak Rijad? She was sure to be the cynosure of all eyes.

"It's only pretend," she murmured, knowing she had to make sure no one else there thought so.

Her hair brushed, her makeup on—she could put it off no longer. She donned the dress. Immediately she experienced the sensuous feelings she'd felt when she'd modeled it for Kharun. The silky material hugged her body like a second skin. The breeze from the veranda caressed her bare back. Slipping on the high heels, she walked to the full-length mirror. The dress made her eyes look silvery. Nervousness gave color to her cheeks. She rubbed her stomach, trying to quell the butterflies. She couldn't help wondering how Kharun would react when he saw her again in the sexiest dress she'd ever owned.

No time like the present to find out.

She grabbed a small, jeweled purse which held her lipstick and headed out, head held high.

Kharun waited for her in the entry, his white dinner jacket fashioned for his wide shoulders. The white jacket might have looked effeminate on other men, but on him it accentuated his rugged masculinity. He looked as daring as a pirate—or a desert raider.

Butterflies danced in her stomach and she had trouble breathing, but she wouldn't let him know. Tilting her chin slightly, she stopped next to him—much closer than she needed to be. Two could play this sensuous game. She almost touched the arm of his jacket, but settled for looking at him from beneath her lashes and smiling.

"You look lovely," he said. Taking her hand in his, he raised it to his lips. Brushing the back with his lips, he turned it slightly until he could brush the sensitive inner skin of her wrist.

Sara felt a shock of desire flood through her. Almost yanking her hand free, she tried to hold her smile. "Is it time to leave?"

"In a moment. I wanted to give you these." He held

out a small jeweler's box.

Sara looked at the box, then at him. "I don't need anything," she said.

"I thought they'd go perfectly with the dress," he replied, still holding out the box.

Gingerly she took and opened it. Inside were two lovely diamond pendant earrings. They would go perfectly with the diamonds in the neck of the dress.

She opened her mouth to refuse them already handing the box back, but he shook his head.

"You'd please me if you'd wear them tonight."

She debated, her gaze drawn to their beauty.

"I have my image to keep up, you know," he said, teasing her.

Or was he teasing? He was a fabulously wealthy man who'd recently married and would ordinarily be doting on a new wife.

She nodded and put them on. Part of the charade.

She couldn't help but wish it was real.

"There, happy?" she asked, tilting her chin so her hair fell back and displayed the danging earrings.

He inclined his head, the amusement in his eyes disturbing her.

So much for trying to maintain a sophisticated veneer. She turned to head for the door and heard him catch his breath. The sound gave her a smidgen of satisfaction—he was still affected by the dress. Good. She hated to be the only one lost in a fog.

The limousine swiftly transported them to the British embassy. The old building was made of stone, with tall columns holding a wide portico in front. Lights shone from all the many ground-floor windows. As they left the limousine, they could hear the murmur of voices and soft background music wafting out on the warm evening air.

Without time to even think, Sara was whisked up the stairs and into the huge reception hall. The short receiving line consisted of the ambassador and his wife and a high-ranking official from England.

Show time, Sara thought. She slipped her hand onto Kharun's arm. He bent his arm and held her hand close to his body. Head held high, she stepped out and the evening began.

An hour later Sara thought her face would crack from smiling so much. She'd swear she'd met everyone in the room and answered so many questions about how she and Kharun met that she wished she'd printed up cards to hand out.

Kharun stayed by her side, giving her snippets of information about the people she met before he exchanged greetings with them. He seemed to know everyone, she thought, wondering how much longer the evening would last. She longed for the privacy of her room.

To add to the strain, she made every effort to play the part of adoring bride. Why had she ever thought she wanted a career in acting? It was hard to remember to glance up to Kharun with what she hoped was love in her gaze from time to time. Primarily because she was so busy trying to focus on breathing. His touch seemed to short-circuit her normal functions. His hand rested on her bare back at one point and she almost forgot the question he asked her. When he laced his fingers through hers later in the evening, her breath caught again. At the rate she was going, she would be a basket case by the end of the reception.

"Ah, Your Excellency, I have not yet had the opportunity to meet your charming bride."

Sara turned at the sound of the voice. She took an instant dislike to the man standing beside them. He wasn't tall. His dark gaze narrowed and his sarcasm did not cover his insincerity.

"Garah Sonharh, my wife Sara. Darling, Garah's one of my uncle's most trusted new ministers."

Kharun's voice was neutral, void of any intonation that would give Sara a hint of how he felt about the man. And that in itself was a clue.

The name was familiar—she suddenly remembered. It was after talking with this man that Kharun had come up with the outlandish scheme to marry instead of pretending an engagement.

"How do you do, sir?" she said sweetly, smiling as vapidly as she could. Maybe the acting lessons would come in handy after all. "I'm so delighted to meet you."

Kharun's hand tightened on hers. She resisted looking at him, knowing she might burst into laughter.

Then the seriousness of the matter reasserted itself. This man was an enemy of her husband—and of her father. If he suspected they weren't truly married, he could precipitate that international incident they were trying to avoid.

"Did you get those photographs you wanted for your husband?" Garah asked.

"Photographs? Oh, of the summer villa? Unfortunately there was a misunderstanding about that." Sara looked up at Kharun, hoping her expression looked adoring. "We got it cleared up, though, didn't we, darling?"

Suddenly she looked straight at Garah. "But how did you hear about that?"

Garah inclined his head slightly. "Rumors, only, madam."

"There you are, I've been looking all over for you," Jasmine said. She wore a burgundy gown and looked stunning.

"Minister Sonharh," she included him in her greeting, then smiled at Sara. "Come and meet some friends of mine. Yasife is dying to meet an American. I told her all about you and Kharun's wildly romantic courtship."

"Do not end up gossiping with the women all night long," Kharun said, kissing the back of Sara's hand before releasing his hold. He turned to Garah as the two women left.

"Thanks," Sara said softly, once out of earshot.

Jasmine laughed. "Garah's bite is worse than his bark and that's formidable. He's against everything Kharun wants to do—from the oil deal to improving the infrastructure, to enticing tourists to boost our economy. I don't know why Kharun doesn't prevail upon our uncle to get rid of him," Jasmine said with a frown.

"Have you asked him?"

"He says it's easier to keep an eye on him at the ministerial level than to constantly wonder what the man might be doing behind his back. Come, here's Yasife."

"So, how did your first reception in Kamtansin go?" Kharun asked as they settled in the limousine after bidding their hosts farewell two hours later.

"Better than I expected," Sara admitted. She kicked off her shoes and wiggled her toes. Frowning, she then wrinkled up her face.

"Is something wrong?"

"I thought I'd try to relax my facial muscles. I hope you don't expect a smile out of me for two days. It'll be that long before my cheeks stop aching."

He laughed softly. The sound was like mulled wine on a cold winter's day. It seeped through Sara, warm and intoxicating.

"I hope you don't expect me to remember the names of the four million people I met tonight," she said brightly to cover her reactions.

"It was only a few dozen, and no, for the most part, you'll remember them after seeing them again and again at various functions. There are a few who are personal friends, do remember them, please."

"Who?" She rested her head against the cushions and closed her eyes, listening to Kharun talk. She could listen to his voice from now until forever.

She felt a brush against her cheek. Slowly she opened her eyes. Kharun was leaning over her.

"We're home."

Sara blinked, awareness gradually returning. Awareness of Kharun growing.

"Did I fall asleep?"

"Right when I was telling you about some friends.

I'll have to make sure I don't bore you next time."

"Oh, no, not that!" She sat up, pressing against his shoulder. "I'm sorry. I'm so tired from the strain of the reception—and meeting Garah Sonharh. Jasmine told me about him. He's the real reason we got married, isn't he? He doesn't suspect anything, does he? Jasmine said he was a real thorn in your side."

"I can handle Garah. Come, you can be in bed in only a couple of minutes."

She followed him into the villa and turned to head for her room when he stopped her.

"Your acting was more than adequate for our deception. Thank you for tonight." He leaned closer and kissed her.

Still half-asleep, still remembering the intoxicating effect of his voice in the darkness of the car, Sara stepped into his embrace and his kiss.

The lassitude from her brief nap vanished. Blood began to pound through her veins as his mouth caressed hers as his lips moved persuasively to coax hers into a response. When she parted her lips, his tongue teased her. She returned the favor, relishing the wild freedom she felt when in Kharun's arms.

His hands were warm on her bare back, sending tendrils of pure pleasure through her. She encircled his neck with her arms and tried to get even closer. She could feel the hard length of him against her and savored the differences between them.

She felt as if she were floating.

He ended the kiss, resting his forehead on hers and gazing deep into her eyes when she reluctantly opened them. The fiery passion he kept under strict control was visible in his eyes. The desire he couldn't completely hide sent a shiver of anticipation and reckless abandonment through her.

What would it be like to make love with Kharun?

"You'd better go to bed now, if you wish to sleep alone," his voice said roughly.

Sara hesitated a split second. One part of her didn't want to go to bed alone, but the other part knew it would be a mistake not to. This was a temporary, short-term, marriage-in-name-only, not the prelude to a lifelong commitment.

She nodded, pulled her arms from around his neck and turned, walking swiftly to her room.

"Damn!" he said softly as the door closed behind her. Angrily, he ran the fingers of one hand through his hair, and back to his neck, easing some of the tension. Since when had he become a blasted Boy Scout? He wasn't known for his altruism. He was ruthless in his pursuit of a business deal or in dealing with mistakes at work.

If he'd kept his mouth on hers, they would be in bed together at this very moment. Instead, he remained in the hallway, staring at a blank door as if he hoped for X-ray vision to see through to Sara's room.

She was probably sliding out of that dress now. It clung to her like a second skin, showing off every delectable curve and valley. He wanted to be the one to slip it from her shoulders, to watch it puddle at her feet on the floor, then raise his gaze to see her wearing nothing at all.

Turning before he did something rash, Kharun strode to his own bedroom. What'd possessed him to put her in the room the farthest from his own? What if she needed something in the night?

Like what his consciousness jeered. Someone to tuck her into bed? Someone to soothe away any nightmares?

Someone to kiss her to sleep?

The truth was he wasn't used to denying himself anything. All evening he'd watched for a sign from Sara that she wasn't immune to the sparks that seemed to fill the room whenever the two of them were together.

If he'd seen a single hint, he wouldn't have sent her to bed alone.

But either she was a terrific actress, or she didn't have a clue. Or maybe she didn't feel the attraction he felt, didn't find anything intriguing about him, like he did with her. Perhaps she was counting the days until the oil deal was finalized and she could return to the United States.

For a moment, the thought of Sara returning to America, never returning to Kamtansin, was more than he cared to deal with. He'd better make the most of her stay. Once she left, he'd likely never see her again.

Thirteen

The next morning Kharun ate breakfast alone on the veranda shaded by the villa. He wondered if Sara was deliberately avoiding him, or tired from last night and was sleeping in. He almost went to check. As he gave it more thought, his mother came out.

"Good morning, Kharun," she said, smiling as he rose to greet her. "I hope I'm not visiting too early, but I'm excited about a project I think you'll love." Angelique looked around. "Where's Sara?"

"We went to the embassy reception last night, she's sleeping in this morning."

"No, I'm not. I got a late start," Sara said from the doorway.

Kharun looked at her and schooled his features to hide his reaction. She looked lovely today—her blond hair swirling around her face. Despite her claim to not smile for a week, she was smiling at his mother.

For a moment he was jealous of that smile. Sara never sent one his way like that.

He greeted her formally and held a chair for his mother. Sara went to the far side of the table and sat down before he could reach her.

Aminna entered, carrying a tray of croissants, muffins, and various breads. She placed it in the center of the table, greeting Kharun's mother.

Kharun waited until the women began to eat before asking his mother why she'd come to visit so early.

"I thought it would be the best time to reach you both—before you began work for the day and Sara took off."

"Took off?" He looked at Sara.

She shrugged. "I'm not going anywhere."

"You will once you see what I've brought," Angelique said. She smiled at her son. "You'll love this."

She rose and left the room, returning two minutes later with a handful of photographs.

With a dramatic gesture, she spread them on the table beside Kharun.

He glanced at the pictures and then at his mother. "And they are?"

"The photographs Sara took."

Sara rose to look over Kharun's shoulder at the pictures.

"They're the ones I took when Angelique drove me around Staboul," she explained.

She smiled when she saw the little children crowding around a tourist. "That one came out well."

Kharun studied each one. There weren't many. He looked at his mother. She was brimming with excitement.

"Nice pictures," he said.

"Kharun—they're perfect for use as a tourist draw. What person seeing these wouldn't want to come to visit our country?"

"Tourist draw?" Sara repeated.

"It's one of Kharun's and Jasmine's special projects. They've been assigned unofficially to expand our tourist bureau. We want more visitors to our country—to boost the economy, to share our lovely beaches with those who like to vacation by the sea, to show our historic buildings and offer another attraction for the world traveler. Kharun, don't you see? These are perfect. Sara could take more and work on the website and promo materials we could then send everywhere! And think of the interest because Sara took them."

"I don't know what you mean," Kharun said slowly, but he suspected.

"Thanks to your surprise marriage, you're making headlines in all the world. Facebook, blogs, even tabloids. It's going viral. People are seeking more information! There's a fascination around wealthy men and an aura around those who don't normally seek publicity. Capitalize on it as you always say!"

Sara looked at Angelique in horror. "We're going viral?"

He glanced over and almost smiled at her horrified expression.

"Isn't that what you said initially—once in the public eye privacy vanishes?"

He wanted to brush away the lines her frown caused, caress her cheek, excuse themselves from his mother and take her into another part of the house to kiss and caress and see if he could spark an answering desire in this golden girl.

Instead, he forced himself to look away and give serious consideration to the suggestion his mother made.

He picked up the pictures and studied each one in detail. Two he tossed aside, they were clear but nothing special. But the rest captured his attention. The framing was excellent. The pictures captured what he'd love others to see. Even the kids in the poor section. The ones he wanted to help as he did the outlying villages.

The added money tourists would bring could help finance the improvements his father had tirelessly worked for. As would the oil deal he was trying to conclude.

"Would you be interested in taking more photographs, with that end in view?" he asked Sara.

She blinked and nodded, looking astonished.

Once again he yearned to whisk her away where the two of them could be alone and undisturbed.

Sara took the photographs from Kharun, careful not to touch his fingers, he noticed. He watched as she studied each one in turn. Slowly her smile came out.

"They came out pretty good, didn't they?" She looked up, and he caught the slight catch in her breath when her gaze met his.

Satisfaction swept through. She wasn't as immune to the attraction between them as she'd been pretending. It wasn't one-sided! Wasn't that interesting?

"So you'll do more?" Angelique asked impatiently.

"I'd be delighted, if you think any picture I take would be worth something," Sara said, stepping away as if she'd get burned if she stayed so close to him.

"Jasmine and I have asked our uncle to make it a

priority, but he moves slowly."

"He's a turtle when it comes to change," his mother said. "Oh, the arguments your father and he had!" She smiled mistily, remembering.

"A fresh perspective would be valuable. If you'd let us know what appeals to you about visiting our country, we can capitalize on that for the American market," Kharun said.

Angelique laughed softly. "This will be wonderful. And give Sara something to do while you're working. I thought this was your honeymoon. But if you insist on working during the day, Sara needs something to occupy herself. And what better time than now when everything's fresh and new to her. Once she's lived here for a few decades, it'll be as if she's always been here. At least that's how I feel."

Kharun looked at Sara, his eyes focusing on the color that sprang into her cheeks, the way she shyly looked at him. Only the two of them knew Sara wouldn't be here for decades. In fact, she might only remain another week or two, until the final papers were signed and the oil agreements firmly in place.

Sara glanced away and tried to take a deep breath. As long as she didn't look at Kharun or touch him, or think about him, she could do this. Surely they'd finalize those oil agreements before long and their pretense come to an end—hopefully before she made a complete idiot of herself.

But she couldn't stop the warm glow that filled her at his comments. Kharun liked her photographs. Angelique liked them. She stared at the photos again.

They were good, even she could see that.

Was this something she could build upon? Make a career with photography? Expand on a hobby and make it into something broader than photojournalism? Maybe specialize in scenes for travel websites and blogs?

"I'm happy to take more pictures. It's fun. I know a little about the Internet, so I could work with someone on a website."

"Good, then it's settled," Angelique said in satisfaction, beaming at Sara and Kharun.

Aminna appeared in the doorway. She spoke to Kharun.

"It appears your mother's on the phone, Sara," he said. "You may take it in the hallway if you wish, for privacy."

Aminna held out a portable phone to Sara when she reached the door. She smiled her thanks and continued walking, putting the phone to her ear.

"Mom?"

"Hi, sweetie, how are things going? When are you and Kharun coming to dinner? We'll be returning home in a few days, surely you can spare enough time for one dinner."

"You're going home?"

"As soon as the oil agreements are finalized and your father says that'll be soon. So we need to get together before we leave. Or I'll have to fly halfway around the world to have dinner with my daughter."

"I'll check with Kharun and call you back."

"Any night next week would work for us. And in the meantime, what about lunch—just you and me? I want to know more about you and Kharun. The wedding came as a complete surprise and we haven't talked properly since."

"Sure, Mom, let me check and call you back. I'd like to have lunch."

Not.

How would she keep the truth from her mother, who knew her so well? She'd have to stall or invite Angelique along so there could be no heart-to-heart.

"Oh, one other thing, do you know a Pete Steede?" her mother asked.

Her editor at the newspaper. "Yes. He's my boss. How did you know his name?"

"He's called at least half a dozen times insisting he talk with you. Maybe you better return the call to keep him from leaving any more messages. He's a bit pushy."

Sara almost laughed. Pete was beyond pushy. How like her mother to understate reality.

"I'll call him right away. And once I check with Kharun, I'll let you know about getting together."

She disconnected, then punched in the familiar number at the newspaper. She tried to calculate the time difference. It would be evening there, but she suspected Pete'd still be hanging around.

Sure enough, he picked up on the second ring.

"Where the hell's your story?" he blurted when he heard her voice.

"I don't have a story," Sara replied, explaining how she'd been caught without getting the photographs or interviews.

"Don't give me that, babe, you are the story. Did you

know going over you'd end up married to the guy? Was that part of the plan? Give the details. We're getting killed in the ratings. Every other damn paper out there is scooping us left and right—and one of our reporters is actually part of the scene. Give."

"There's nothing to say, Pete. And I'm quitting. I can't work for you anymore."

"Hey, babe, you owe me. I gave you a job when you had no experience. Gave you a chance to scoop the world with some photo snaps of one of the world's most eligible bachelors. I could've sent someone else. Give with the details! What's it like living in the lap of luxury? Does anyone speak English? Are you in a harem?"

"For heaven's sake, Pete, you make it sound like I've gone back to the Dark Ages. Most of Kamtansin is as modern as Algiers. There're some lovely old mosques and buildings, small tiny streets with a lot of traffic and the people I've met are friendly. I haven't had a chance to do much shopping, but I bet there're some real bargains here. I am not in a harem. Kharun has a beautiful villa right on the Mediterranean Sea."

"So if you're not a prisoner, why not contact me? We've been waiting for a week for some news. That country's hot—with the proposed new oil leases and the potential for more."

"It's also pretty, but some areas are really desperate. That's why the oil leases are so crucial. The income from the leases will enable the society to progress more rapidly. Not that everyone's in agreement about that. But it doesn't matter, family rules over here."

"Your guy's rich, the country's poor, what else?"

"Stop, Pete. I'm not giving a report. I called to tell you to stop calling my mother."

"Give me your number then. I don't like one of my reporters being out of touch."

"Didn't you hear me, I quit! You can't call here." Sara looked up—Kharun stood a short distance away watching her.

"I've got to go, goodbye." She disconnected and looked at him wondering how to explain.

"Your mother's welcome to call anytime she wishes," he said mildly.

Flustered, she tried to smile. Not for anything did she want him to know she was speaking with her editor. He'd be convinced she still planned to do a story!

Fourteen

"Um, my mother wants to know when we're available to have dinner with them," Sara said, hoping her flustered feeling didn't show. "I knew it wouldn't be long before she invited us."

Kharun tilted his head slightly, his eyes studying her. "Whenever you'd like."

"In a couple of days, then?"

"Fine. You took longer than I expected. My mother needs to leave soon , and she wishes to discuss your taking more pictures focused on a campaign for promoting our country."

"Do you think I can take that quality of pictures? Wouldn't a professional be better?"

"What do you think?"

She almost held her breath. Had she finally found something she was good at?

"I'd give it my best. But I'm really a novice at this. Photography has always been a hobby."

"The high quality of the pictures is perfect. The composition and artistic eye that captures the essence of what you see and captures it makes them fabulous— especially for the tourist trade. Your perspective will differ from another's, but there's no denying the focal point in the pictures you already took."

"You're bolstering my courage to try."

"That's within you, Sara. Come and arrange things with my mother. I have work to do. Shall we ride this afternoon at five?"

"I'd like that."

The day passed swiftly. Angelique called Jasmine to discuss the possibilities of Sara working with her. Jasmine said she'd be glad to discuss the idea with Sara. When Angelique left for Staboul, Sara caught a ride to the Rijad Industries headquarters.

Meeting with Jasmine was an eye-opener for Sara.

The tall building in the heart of the business section housed several businesses owned and run by the Rijad family, from shipping lines to oil exploration to import-export. Jasmine headed that branch herself.

"Mother said you'd help with the idea we have of trying to expand the tourist trade," Jasmine said closing her office door behind Sara when she arrived.

Glancing around the lavishly appointed office, Sara was suddenly envious. She'd had a tiny cubbyhole of space at the newspaper. Nothing like the splendid view Jasmine had, nor the solid furnishings or artwork on the walls. The carpet beneath her feet was thicker than in her apartment at home!

Jasmine looked at her warily. "What's the real scoop?"

"I'm glad to do what I can. Your mother seemed to think my pictures turned out really good, but I don't know anything about luring tourists."

"How long do you plan to stay here? Once the leases are signed, you'll return to America. I don't think my mother would have suggested the idea if she knew the real circumstances".

Sara turned to face her. "If it's something I can do, I would commit to seeing it through—no matter when the oil leases are signed."

Jasmine studied her for a minute.

Sara was uncomfortable, but spurred on by the comments Kharun had made, she wanted to try this—more than anything she'd tried before.

"I don't know much about luring tourists, however," she confessed.

Jasmine shrugged, moving behind her desk and sitting. "Neither do we! But it's something my father supported. Kharun and I have badgered our uncle tirelessly until he finally told us to do what we wanted. Carte Blanche's great, except that we don't have any idea on how to proceed. I have one person working flat out on the website. You'll be perfect for telling us what would appeal to an American tourist—you're so new here."

"That's what your mother said. I have to say, before my father became involved with the oil leases, I hadn't heard anything about your country."

Jasmine made a face. "So true for everyone, I suspect. We're small, politically unimportant. Which also gives us stability other Arab countries don't have. So that's a good place to start. Come, I'll introduce you to Tamil. Between the two of you, maybe we can really get going."

Jasmine's enthusiasm was contagious.

Sara felt excited for the first time since she started work at the newspaper with such high hopes.

Yet as she followed Jasmine to a lower floor, she began to question what she was doing. Her stay in Kamtansin wouldn't be lengthy. Once her marriage to Kharun ended, she really had no reason to remain—unless it proved to be more than a temporary position to keep her busy while she was here.

She followed when Jasmine stepped into an office and introduced Sara to Tamil.

Sara was relieved to discover he spoke English though rather slowly. It would facilitate working together since she spoke no Arabic.

By the end of the afternoon, Sara's head was swimming with ideas and plans. The three of them discussed various strategies and ambitions; jotted pages of notes; and arranged to meet the next day to take a tour. Jasmine and Tamil had ideas of what they considered the most appealing aspects of the city. They wanted to get Sara's opinions.

Angelique's driver drove her back to the villa.

Once out of the car, she rang the doorbell and the same maid who let her in before opened the door. She smiled and again said something to Sara.

"Probably telling me to get a key," Sara murmured as she headed for her room. Glancing at her watch, she saw it was almost five. If she wanted to be on time for her ride with Kharun, she'd better change in a hurry.

She was bubbling with all she wanted to share. As she donned her jeans, she almost laughed. They'd act like a regular married couple—telling each other about their day.

Except—Kharun didn't tell her about his day. Did he still suspect she was a spy? How absurd. Maybe if she tried —

Tried what? She sat on the edge of her bed.

What did she want? To get to know Kharun better?

Theirs was a temporary arrangement. She agreed to it to avoid scandal and make sure the oil treaties weren't jeopardized. They'd already discussed an annulment once the leases were signed. There was no long term to consider.

She glanced around her room and then out at the garden, taking a deep breath. The fragrance of the flowers was light, mingling with that of the warm sea air. Her restlessness wasn't as strong when she was here. The setting was idyllic. And despite the suspicions Kharun seemed to hold, she enjoyed being with him.

And liked his kisses.

Whoa, don't go there!

She jumped up and finished changing, hurrying to the stables as if trying to flee her own thoughts.

The groom had already saddled the horses. Kharun was talking with him. When he heard Sara, he turned and watched her walk to the stable.

"Ready?"

"Yes."

They followed the trail to the beach, Sara in the lead. Alia was prancing impatiently, anxious for the run she expected.

"Beat you!" Sara called, tearing down the beach. She

could hear Kharun following, the pounding hoofs of Satin Magic drawing closer every moment. Laughing in exhilaration, Sara urged Alia faster. The wind blew through her hair, the sea sparkled like diamonds in the sun.

This is what she should capture to lure tourists. The sheer joy would entice even the most jaded traveler. How could she convey this feeling to the world?

Satin Magic was gaining. He was a strong horse, with a longer stride. Sara knew she couldn't keep her lead, but she and Alia would give it their best. Soon they were neck and neck, then Satin Magic pulled ahead.

Sara began to ease Alia down into a slower gait until they were trotting. Kharun slowed, turned and came back to where they were.

"You win!" Sara called.

He was grinning as he fell into step with her. "Next time, I'll win quicker with an equal start. I take it by your absence all day that you and Jasmine agreed to work together?"

"Tamil and I will be working on the project. Jasmine will oversee it. We have so many ideas. He's traveled quite a bit, and so have I. We each have ideas on what we look for and what's appealing. We need to explore hotels and restaurants and see who's ready for an influx of foreign travelers. See what tours we might devise. Decide where to target our campaign initially. There's so much to do!"

Excited with all the ideas tumbling in her mind, she wanted to share with Kharun. She related every idea discussed—from their plans to visit the various sights in the city of Staboul, to interviewing hotel managers, to testing restaurants.

She was unaware of how her eyes sparkled in excitement or how the color flooded her cheeks from her ride. He liked watching the expressions chasing across her face.

"Of course, what would make it perfect would be a desert trip. It's so different from what most of the world knows, I'm sure it'd be a draw unto itself."

He looked at her. "You like the desert?"

"Except for my foray to try to photograph your retreat, I've never been."

She patted Alia's neck. "The thought of riding a horse along the dunes has a lot of appeal. The oasis where the jail was rose so unexpectedly from the barren land. I imagine it could appear almost romantic given the proper preparation. And you have to admit it'd differ greatly from what most European and Americans are used to—always supposing there's enough water and shade to support a tour group."

"Sometimes I go beyond the oasis. Satin Magic and I spend days on the desert. It's cleansing. Rejuvenating, yet relaxing."

She nodded. "I'd love to see that sometime," she said wistfully. "But this is nice, riding along the sea. Look, there are pleasure boats out today. I haven't noticed them before—only the big ships out on the horizon."

He glanced at the two boats apparently at anchor a few hundred yards from the shore. "Another feature you can include. For those who sail the Med, we can offer docking facilities. We already have a couple of large marinas in Staboul. Others could be built."

"How about docks large enough for pleasure cruises?"

"Ah, you think big. We could convert one or two of our deep water docks from freight, I suppose."

"I can't wait to talk to Tamil about that! So I told you about my day, how was yours?" she asked daringly. They turned the horses for home. She liked the ride back each afternoon, it was slower, took longer and allowed them to talk—just the two of them. For a few minutes each day she could forget he didn't trust her.

For a while it was only Kharun and Sara.

She admired how he sat on his horse. His dark hair gleamed in the sunshine, his shoulders broad and strong. Savoring the image, she burned it into her memory. She never wanted to forget a single minute with him.

"I didn't realize your family operated so many businesses. Jasmine runs the import-export firm. Do you oversee them all?"

"You didn't know?" he asked.

Suspiciously, she thought.

She shook her head. "I was very impressed," she said. "I thought you helped out your uncle with the oil leases and other projects he needed done."

"My father started two of the firms. His father had begun the oil leases. Jasmine and I started the import-export. She assumed full control when our father died. By then I was heavily involved in the shipping lines, and now oversee the oil company, as well. It's a family concern. Some cousins participate as well. And my mother takes an interest though not an active role."

"No wonder you work all the time," she murmured.

"When a person enjoys what he does, it's not a hardship."

"What do you do for fun?" Sara asked as they neared the path leading back to the stables. Was their ride coming to an end so soon? She wanted to cling to the moments, stretch them out.

"I enjoy riding."

"How about swimming? You've never gone once since I've been here. Living right by the sea, having that lovely pool, I'd think you'd take advantage of the water."

"Ah, but I do. I usually swim first thing in the mornings while you're still sleeping."

"Oh."

They turned into the path, going single file, Kharun in the lead. Sara wondered if it would look suspiciously obvious if she arose early the next morning and happened to wish to go swimming.

"Do you ever swim at night?" she called.

He looked over his shoulder, his dark eyes enigmatic. "Sometimes. Want to go tonight?"

Her heart skipped a beat. She nodded.

"After dinner, we can take a walk. If the warmth holds, we'll swim in the sea," he said. His voice was rife with sensual promise, his eyes captivating.

Sara felt the heat rise in her cheeks, but smiled slowly, hoping the sheer joy she felt didn't show. "I'd like that."

Sara wondered if their walk would still take place when they reached the house and found Piers waiting for

Kharun.

"It's late," Kharun said when greeting his friend and adviser. "Couldn't whatever you're here for have waited until morning?"

Piers shrugged, looked at Sara. "You never minded before."

"Things change," Kharun answered shortly. He lifted Sara's hand and kissed it blatantly. "Change for dinner. I'll see to Piers."

Sara was aware of the men watching her as she headed for her wing of the house. She paused once around the bend in the pathway and stopped.

She couldn't understand what Piers said, but from his tone, she suspected it was a warning.

She knew he didn't trust her.

How did Kharun really feel? If she knew Arabic, she might have heard something that would tell her.

With a sigh, she continued to her room.

Kharun closed the door to his office. "Do you have reasons for thinking she's here to spy? A woman who speaks no Arabic and has yet to ask one question about our position on the oil leases?"

"It's odd she showed up at this particular time, that's all."

Kharun shrugged. "What's so important you have to come this late?"

"I believe the Americans have agreed to your last counteroffer. We should go over it all in great detail, but I believe we are almost ready for you to send contracts to your uncle for his approval."

Kharun nodded, his expression showing no

emotion.

It was too soon. He shook his head. They'd been working on this deal for weeks now. The new leases would mean a great deal to his country.

But it would also mean the need to stay married to Sara would end.

And he wasn't ready for that. Not yet.

"I thought you'd be elated," Piers murmured, drawing out the thick folder from his briefcase.

"I'm pleased," Kharun said. "But let's make sure before we celebrate. No use anticipating."

But it was clear when he read the counteroffer acceptance that the contracts were almost ready to be print and signed.

"It doesn't look like anything Sara could have told her father has changed either position on this," Kharun said.

"Doesn't mean they didn't try, that's all I'm saying. So, is it an annulment, or divorce?"

Kharun looked at his friend, his eyes cold and hard. "You'll be one of the first to know—when the time's right."

"Sorry, I didn't mean to overstep my bounds," Piers said hastily.

Fifteen

Kharun was still considering the question, and the possible answer when he changed for dinner. He had Aminna set the table on the patio overlooking the garden. After dinner, he and Sara would take that walk along the beach and maybe go swimming.

The more he grew to know her, the more she fascinated him. Was it her quicksilver mind, flitting from one topic to another that entertained? Or was it the way she had of looking at him sometimes as if he was the most important person in the world that he found so enticing? Or was it that air of innocence she portrayed so well?

Maybe Piers had been correct, she'd agreed to the fake marriage as a way to seduce him into revealing secrets.

Yet she'd made no overt attempts at seduction. He wanted to believe she'd been honest in her commitment to avoid scandal. Nothing so far had shown him differently.

Sara dressed with care for dinner. The sun dress she donned was her favorite, loose and flowing, yet clinging as she walked, displaying her figure to full advantage. She felt she needed all the advantage she could get. Time was growing short.

She'd resented being forced into this marriage of convenience. But it turned out to be much more pleasant than she'd expected. Granted, she'd change a few things if she could. But for the most part she was resigned to the mock marriage to avoid any scandal, especially as it would have reflected so poorly on her father.

She hadn't counted on developing such an interest in Kharun.

Would he want to continue to see her after they parted?

A pang struck her. What if he didn't?

"All the more reason to make memories while I can," she said, staring at herself in the mirror. She dabbed on a hint of perfume and recapped the bottle. Taking a deep breath, she turned and headed for dinner.

A most romantic setting, she thought, stepping into the patio after Aminna told her where to find Kharun when she found the dining room empty.

Discreet lighting gave soft illumination. The breeze died down. The air was redolent with the fragrance of roses. And the soft murmur of the sea made a soft, melodic background.

The small table was set with gleaming silverware, sparkling crystal. Candles shimmered, their flames dancing, reflected in Kharun's dark eyes.

"You look lovely," he said softly, reaching out his hand.

Sara slipped hers into his, feeling the shock of awareness that always took her by surprise when he touched her. Her heart pounded and her skin grew tight with sensitivity and longing.

"Let's eat, then we'll take that walk along the beach," he said, seating her.

Dinner flew by. Sara was aware of every second, wondering what the future held. Not endless days ahead, but later tonight. Would their walk draw them even closer? Would he kiss her again?

She could scarcely eat, despite the wonderful aromas and tastes of the meal Aminna had prepared.

Kharun spoke of cities he'd visited when he lived in America and she told him about growing up with a father who traveled the world. They shared their favorite places in Paris. And their love for riding, arguing the various merits of different breeds of horses.

By the time they finished eating, she was a bundle of nerves. Always in the back of her mind was the promised walk.

Kharun looked at her gravely. "What's wrong?"

"Nothing."

He didn't look as if the answer satisfied, so she continued. "I'm still excited about the plans Tamil and I made today. I can't wait until tomorrow when we look around the city."

He nodded, his eyes narrowed. "Shall we take that walk?"

She blew out her breath and smiled. "I'd like that."

The moon was full, providing enough light to see the path, bathing the white sand in its glow. Sara stopped when they reached the beach to slip off her sandals.

"I like going barefoot," she said, looping them with

one finger.

"Be careful where you step. There are broken shells sometimes," he warned, taking her free hand.

She almost shivered at the sensations that tingled along her arm at his touch.

Glancing around, she almost didn't recognize the beach as the same place she'd visited several mornings.

An air of mystery hovered. The sea was dark, the anchor lights of the pleasure crafts in the distance the only break in the blackness. The silvery sheen of the sand added to her pleasure, evoking dreams of romantic settings and faithful lovers.

Kharun began angling toward the water.

"I think I'd come out every night if I lived here," Sara murmured.

"You do live here."

"Temporarily." She flicked him a quick glance. "How are the lease discussions coming?"

He hesitated a moment. She glanced at him.

"They're progressing. How does your father feel about them?"

"I don't know. I haven't spoken to him since our wedding. I talked to my mother again and arranged for us to have dinner with them tomorrow night if that's all right with you. Will that be awkward—you and my father sitting down to dinner when you are on opposite sides of negotiations?"

"We are not enemies. We both want these leases, we're still working on the details."

"Mom doesn't like business discussions at the table," she warned.

"A wise woman. I enjoyed meeting her. Are you worried about having dinner with them?"

"A bit. What if they suspect this is all a sham?"

"What would happen?"

She sighed. "They'd be disappointed. I'm a trial to them."

"I doubt it. From what I saw, they seemed to delight in your company."

"That's because you saw them at the wedding— when they were happy. Someone else took me off their hands."

"Do you really think they feel that way? At first they seemed bewildered with the speed of the wedding. But when they thought you were happy, they became happy."

"So they'll be even more disappointed when the truth comes out. Not that that's your worry."

"We don't have to end the marriage the day we sign the agreements, you know," he said slowly.

"We don't?"

Kharun stopped and turned her so she faced him. He released her hand and placed his on her shoulders.

"Piers suggested it might be a slap in the face to the ministers to end it immediately by annulment. We'd be essentially telling them all we'd played a trick."

"Oh."

For some reason his rationale depressed her.

She'd thought when he first spoke he wanted to keep their arrangement a little longer. Now it was to further expediency, nothing more.

"So what do you think?" he asked.

"Whatever."

She couldn't think with Kharun's hands toying with her hair, his thumbs caressing her jaw. She could only feel the myriad sensations that filled her that heated her blood and had her longing for things unknown.

"I was thinking—"

"What?" She tried breathing normally, every nerve cell at attention and craving more.

"Maybe an annulment isn't such a good idea. A divorce would be more persuasive."

Her heart pounded so hard she wondered if he could see it. Blood pulsed like thunder through her veins. She peered up at him, trying to determine what he was saying—what he really meant.

"A divorce?"

"It's the customary way to end a marriage that has been consummated," he said, leaning in to kiss her.

Sixteen

He was kissing her and all she could think of was he wanted more. More than kisses.

Rational thought fled as touch turned her knees wobbly and her thought processes to mush.

He wanted her. Every brush of his lips, stroke of his tongue, caress of his fingertips shouted the message loud and clear.

And she wanted him. Wanted to be closer still, to explore all the cravings that filled her body. Wanted to touch him all over, learn every secret he had.

When he pulled back to look at her, she smiled. "I think a divorce is the only way to go," she said huskily.

He swept her up into his arms, her strong desert raider, and turned for the house. She encircled his neck, cherishing every moment. What woman didn't dream of a man sweeping her off her feet since seeing Rhett sweep Scarlet up the steps in *Gone With the Wind*? Was anything more romantic?

Only to have it happen to her.

She scarcely noticed when they reached the garden, except she could see him better with the illumination of the garden lights. He followed the path to her room, entering through the opened French doors.

The soft twinkling from the pathway lights gave all the light they needed. Setting her beside the bed, he took her sandals and dropped them on the floor.

"Are you sure, Sara? There'll be no going back," he said, caressing her cheek.

Her heart exploded with love for this enigmatic man before her. She didn't know him well, but she knew he was honorable and caring. Theirs was an odd arrangement, doomed to end before long. But she loved him as she'd never loved another.

When had that happened?

Could the feelings she had truly be love?

Yet what was more natural than a woman wanting to share all she could with the man she loved?

"I'm very sure, Kharun." So saying, she reached up and pulled his head down for a kiss.

Taking liberties she would never have dared even a day before, she threaded her fingers in his thick hair, relishing her right to touch him.

His hands roamed over her back, pressing her against his hard body, lifting her slightly to bring her even closer. Heat built as his clever fingers found the fastenings for her dress and released them. The cool air on her back should have startled, but she enthralled in the roiling sensations that grew with each feather stroke of his fingers.

The world spun when he lifted her to place her on the bed. Then it righted itself as he joined her.

Sara awoke when Kharun left. Dawn was breaking. He was going for his swim, she knew. For an instant, she considered throwing back the light covering and joining him. But tendrils of passion still filled her and she wanted to savor the feelings a bit longer. She smiled dreamily and drifted back to sleep hugging the pillow he'd used, breathing in his scent.

By the time Sara awoke for the day, the sun was high in the sky. Slowly she bathed and dressed. Wondering where Kharun was, she headed for the dining room. She was disappointed to find it empty. One place was set at the table and some food warmed on the sideboard. She poured a cup of coffee and selected a couple of croissants. Carrying her light breakfast, she went outside to sit in the shady veranda.

Last night had been beyond her wildest dreams. They'd made love more than once and each time was as if the act of love had been invented solely to join Kharun and Sara forever.

Wryly she acknowledged he likely didn't feel the same way. The thought threatened to overwhelm her with sadness. It was enough she'd had one night with him.

Maybe she'd have more nights in the short time remaining.

She'd entered this arrangement fully aware of the reasons and outcome. She'd see her commitment through and leave when the time came.

She hoped she was able to leave without clinging, without asking for more than Kharun ever promised to give.

Aminna stepped into the doorway.

"His Excellency said to tell you he had to go to the

city today. He'll meet you at the hotel for dinner with your parents at seven."

Sara tried to smile, but her hopes and dreams vanished in an instant. Confirmation that last night hadn't meant as much to him as it had to her. Not with such a cryptic message. Not with leaving her alone all day. Leaving without even seeking her out to say goodbye in person.

Without another kiss.

"Thank you. I'll be going to the city myself today."

At least she had the meeting with Tamil to look forward to. How she would have faced the day without that, she didn't know.

"What time? I'll inform the driver," Aminna asked.

"I need to be at the company headquarters at ten."

Aminna bowed slightly and left Sara to her rueful thoughts.

By the time seven o'clock that evening rolled around, Sara had been through more emotional turmoil than she cared to repeat. She vacillated from trying to understand the demands of Kharun's work to being convinced he'd used it as a mere excuse to avoid her.

She went up to her parents' suite and knocked on the door a few minutes before seven. Might as well get this over with and hope for the best.

"Sara!" Her mother swept her into her arms for a brief hug, then held her back, studying her daughter.

"You look radiant."

Startled, Sara glanced at the nearby mirror. Did she? Or was her mother seeing only what she wanted to see?

"You look exactly like a new bride should look. I'm

so happy for you, sweetie. Come in and tell me all about being married to Kharun. I imagine he's vastly different from your father."

"One type A personality's similar to another," Sara said, smiling at her mother.

"Ah, but your father wasn't always like that. We married right out of college. We were both so young when he started building his company. But Kharun's already well established—not only in running several international businesses, but negotiating oil treaties on behalf of his country. Vastly different from the early days of our marriage."

"I guess," Sara said, struck by the difference.

They moved into the sitting room area of the suite and settled on the luxurious sofas.

"Before I forget, though I doubt there's a danger of that, your obnoxious boss keeps calling, demanding to talk to you. He's really getting annoying."

"Pete? I called him after you told me of his calls. He's still bothering you?"

"Persistent, I have to give him that."

"Ignore him. Hang up the next time he calls, maybe that'll get through to him," Sara said. She was a bit annoyed herself to know the man kept calling her mother.

"Actually, I have the front desk screening our calls now. I haven't spoken directly with him today. Ah, here's your father."

"Sara." Samuel Kinsale entered from the adjoining room. He hugged her when she rose, then held her away from him, his hands on her shoulders, studying her.

"Marriage seems to agree with you," he said. Glancing around, he frowned. "Where's Kharun?"

A tap sounded at the outer door.

"That's probably him now. He was coming from the office," Sara said, crossing to the door. Her heart skipped a beat in anticipation.

She opened the door, struck anew by Kharun's sexy looks. Her breath caught when he swept her into his arms and kissed her deeply. When he pulled back a moment later, she wanted to grab hold and never let go.

Startled by the trend of her thoughts, she smiled shakily and stepped back, as if putting distance between them could erase her foolish desires.

"Hi," she said breathlessly.

He smiled that lazy smile that took her breath away He then looked beyond her to her parents.

"Good evening."

"Kharun, good to see you," Sam said, greeting their guest with obvious warmth. Before long, Roberta had everyone sitting on the sofas, comfortable and at ease.

"No talking shop tonight," she warned. "This is a family dinner, not some negotiating session!"

Samuel laughed and nodded. "Very well. Kharun and I bow to your wishes. Tell me, how are you enjoying married life?" he asked Kharun.

Kharun glanced at Sara then looked at her father. "It's different from what I expected, but it has its compensations."

She pasted an insipid smile on her face and hoped her thoughts weren't reflected. Marriage wasn't what he expected because theirs was a farce. He deserved to marry a woman he cared about, not to cover up a potential scandal that might prove an embarrassment to his country.

The comment about compensation didn't go unnoticed. Was that all last night had been to him, a form of compensation for the sacrifice he'd made?

Her head held high, Sara tried to maintain the facade of a radiant bride, happy with life. But she longed for privacy. Even her room at Kharun's villa would be preferable to being with her parents now trying to keep up appearances with people who knew her so well.

Kharun didn't help matters. He sat much too close. She could feel his thigh against hers, and his shoulder brushed hers when he put his arm around her shoulders. His hand lightly traced circles against the sensitive skin of her upper arm.

She could hardly concentrate on the conversation. Every fiber of her being resonated to the sensations sweeping through from his touch. How was anyone supposed to remain coherent when all they could think about was getting alone with the man and seeing if they could take up where they'd left off the night before?

She flicked a quick look at her mother. Roberta was serenely responding to one of Kharun's questions. She didn't seem to notice anything amiss. Sara felt sure the entire world could hear her rapid heartbeat, feel the heat that suffused, know she was focused on Kharun to the exclusion of everything else.

Dinner was served on the table near the window in the suite. The hotel sent the best wait staff to see to their every need.

Delightful as it was, to Sara it seemed interminable. She kept her eyes on her plate, lest she give away her emotional turmoil and stare at Kharun for endless moments like a puppy. Once or twice, when addressed directly, she looked up. Each time Kharun's warm gaze rested on her.

It was all for show. To put on a good front before her parents, to pretend to the world that everything was fine.

Suddenly Sara wished with all her heart it wasn't a charade. That they married for all the usual reasons. And planned to stay married forever. She longed to go home together when the evening ended and close the rest of the world out of their special place.

She stared at the last of the food on her plate wryly admitting to the fact that she'd fallen in love with a man who didn't trust her! A man who found her a problem to be dealt with and then summarily dismissed once the situation was resolved. And it was all her fault. Trying to take forbidden pictures wasn't the best move she'd ever made. Nothing had gone the way she'd expected since she stepped foot onto Kamtansin soil.

She reached for her water and took a long drink, wishing she could catch the next plane home.

She couldn't stay. She'd give herself away any instant and she couldn't bear the humiliation of his knowing the awkward, flaky daughter of Samuel Kinsale had fallen in love with one of the world's richest men.

At least when she made mistakes, they were terrific ones. No little namby-pamby ones for her.

She should have been better prepared. She should

have guarded her heart, put up barriers against his appeal and attraction.

What she should have done was refused to go riding with him that first time, ignored his family, fought him at every turn and continually pushed to leave.

Now she never wanted to leave, yet the days were counting down, and it was only a matter of time before he'd ask her to. Their marriage facade would no longer be necessary once the leases were final. Her ideas for tourism might be used, but her presence wouldn't be required.

She could hardly keep from jumping up and screaming at the unfairness of it all. For the first time she'd found someone she truly loved, and he didn't love her in return.

"Are you all right?" Kharun asked.

Sara looked up. "Fine."

His eyes narrowed as he studied her. Thankfully, she knew he couldn't read minds. But his steady regard made her nervous.

She wasn't fine. She'd made the biggest mess of her life. But she'd bluff her way through. The entire sequence of events was her fault. She wouldn't add to it by letting him suspect her feelings had changed.

The evening seemed endless. Finally it was time to leave.

Her mother gave her a hug. "I like him so much. I hope you'll always be happy."

Sara smiled, feeling as if a knife was twisting in her heart. What would her mother say in a few weeks when the marriage was over?

Sara didn't even want to think about it. She knew they'd blame her and once again wonder where they'd gone wrong.

"You were silent tonight," Kharun said as they settled in the limousine and headed for the villa. "Are you usually so quiet around your parents?"

"What? Oh, no. We talk a lot, actually."

"So I was the damper on the evening?"

She shook her head, trying to see him in the darkness. The ride reminded her of that first ride from the jail in the desert. She'd never in a million years suspected she'd end up loving the man beside her.

When they reached the villa, Kharun held out his hand to assist her from the car. He didn't release it and Sara tried unsuccessfully to tug free. She didn't need any closer proximity to the man. Distance was what she needed.

Lights were on when they entered providing a soft illumination in the living room and halls.

Kharun raised her hand to his lips, brushing a tantalizing kiss to her wrist. "Stay the night with me," he said, his voice low and husky.

It was as if liquid heat poured through her. *He wanted her again tonight!*

Dare she follow through?

She loved him, she wanted to be with him in every way. But theirs was only a temporary alliance. Could she spend the night with him and protect her heart?

The heartache would come either way. Why not grab the chance to be with him?

"Your place or mine?" she asked.

"Tonight, mine."

He leaned over to kiss her. His mouth touched hers with a familiarity that belied the short time they'd known each other. The sensations that filled her were growing familiar with each passing second. She opened her lips to deepen their kiss, thrilled at the responsiveness he displayed.

Slowly, as if dancing to some unheard tune, he turned her and moved with easy abandonment down the long hall, away from her room and the illusion of safety it provided.

Instead, between kisses, she knew they were going to a room she'd yet to see. Kharun's private retreat.

When they reached the door, it stood ajar. Sara loosened her arms, locked around his neck, and peered into the dimness. She saw a bed and the gleam of light on one wall—a mirror reflecting the hallway illumination.

She looked up into Kharun's dark gaze—alive with desire and impatience, though he kept the latter in check.

"Yes or no?" he said, as if divining her uncertainty.

He was giving the choice to her.

"Yes." She reached up and kissed him, trying to let him know by touch and actions how much she wanted him. How much she reveled being with him. If she could offer nothing else, she'd be honest in this.

And if it had to end, then she'd make sure it ended gloriously.

Maybe down through the years, Kharun would think of her once in a while—and think of what might have been.

The next morning Kharun woke early. Sara snuggled next to him, sound asleep. For a long moment he watched her, fascinated by the hint of color in her cheeks, the sweep of her lashes against her fair skin. Slowly he ran his fingers through her hair, enjoying the shimmering color and satiny softness. For a moment he thought he could spend the entire day watching Sara sleep.

Then reality took hold. He had a meeting at nine and things to see to before that. This was not the time or the place to indulge in fantasies—no matter how tempting.

Once the oil leases were resolved, however, he'd find the time and place to discover more about this bewitching woman who was his wife.

Piers was waiting for him when he reached the downtown offices, his face beaming.

"I think you'll be pleased with the lease terms. We've gotten everything we asked for on the last go. I'd say we're ready to sign. Your uncle's pleased. He said to tell you, he's ready to sign if you give him the go-ahead."

"Good work."

"Not that I want to take anything away from your negotiating skills, but marrying Sara was a stroke of genius. I'm sure some of the concessions we got were a result of her father's feeling generous in light of the marriage," Piers said.

Kharun frowned. He didn't want favors like that.

The relationship between him and Sara was complex. They were both walking a fine line. And after last night, and the night before, the line had blurred.

Now it looked like a quick finish to the business at hand.

Was he ready for that? The necessity for their marriage would vanish. No matter how much Garah and Hamin wished to discredit the oil deal with his uncle, once the leases were signed, it would prove a moot point.

Kharun's phone rang.

"Yes?" His secretary was on the other end. Hearing the news that Garah Sonharh was in the outer office demanding to see him, he told her to send him in.

"I suspect Garah has heard the news," he said as he hung up.

Piers looked puzzled. "He's here?"

Garah pushed open the door, pausing in the opening for dramatic impact.

"You are a fool, Kharun. It wasn't enough you wished to jeopardize the future of our country, but to make it possible for the paparazzi to hold us to ridicule is beyond acceptable."

He strode into the office and tossed several faxed newspaper articles on the desk.

Kharun looked at the top one. It was from a tabloid newspaper from the United States. A bad photo of Sara stared back at him. The headlines screamed A Hostage To Fortune?

He looked up. "What's this, Garah?"

"Copies of newspapers on sale in the United States. One of the people in the embassy saw it, copied it and sent it to me. If your new wife isn't a spy, then she certainly is a woman to make the most of her opportunities. In this case, fame and notoriety on a worldwide scale. I cannot help but think your uncle will think twice about signing any lease with a member of the opposition so bent on ridiculing us."

"I'll deal with it," Kharun said evenly. He wanted to smash something—preferably Garah's face.

But that would solve nothing. He glanced at the paper again—he'd need to read the newspaper article, assess the damage, then rectify the situation.

But not with Garah still in the room.

"I'm taking copies to your uncle," Garah said.

"You must do what you think's right, of course," Kharun said disinterestedly.

He looked at Piers.

"I'll see you out," Piers said, quick to catch on.

Kharun watched as Piers hustled Garah from his office.

Once the door shut behind them, he sat down and drew the damaging fax papers toward him. The second sheet showed pictures of them racing on the beach. The caption read "Aborted escape attempt."

He almost laughed. The photographer had caught their moment where Sara had initially been leading. A second picture showed them stopped, his hand on her arm.

The next showed them on the beach. He remembered that night, the fragrance she wore that'd filled him with such desire. Her laughter and her delight in wading in the warm sea. When she'd almost stepped on a broken shell, he'd caught her and pulled her back. From a distance, and with the wrong interpretation, he guessed it could look as if she were trying to escape and that he'd stopped her.

It had to have been the pleasure crafts anchored off the beach—a clever cover for the paparazzi.

He set the sheet aside and began to read the inflaming article. Had Sara sent this in? If enough people read it and believed it, it could damage their standing with the United States.

From the first moment, she'd been trouble.

He pushed back his chair and rose. Time to get this settled once and for all.

Seventeen

Sara sat on the patio beside the pool sipping her last cup of coffee for the morning. The air was soft against her skin, a hint of the sea mingled with the faint fragrance of the flowers. She sat beneath an umbrella which shaded her from the sun. Later she was due to meet Tamil for more discussions. But right now she had nothing to do.

Except dream.

And remember.

Remember the most incredible night of her life. She wondered if Kharun had any idea how sexy he was. Or how merely thinking about him could set her senses spinning. Did the memory of their loving spring to mind when he was at work or were men better able to compartmentalize their lives?

"Telephone for you," Aminna said in her heavily accented French, standing in the doorway.

Sara smiled and rose, glancing around for the portable phone. She didn't see it.

"Where shall I take it?"

"In the office." She led the way.

Sara slipped into Kharun's office and saw the phone

receiver lying on the desk. Aminna nodded and left, shooing out the maid who'd been dusting.

"Hello?" She sank into the big chair behind the desk, feeling odd to be in Kharun's office with him not there.

"Sara, it's your mother."

"Is something wrong?"

She could tell by the tone in her mother's voice something was definitely wrong.

"Your father received a call from a friend of his in the State Department asking if you were all right."

"Why in the world would he get such a call?"

"Apparently because of two newspaper articles that appeared across the U.S. yesterday."

Sara felt her blood grow cold. "What kind of articles?"

"Headlines implying you're being held hostage while the oil leases are being negotiated."

She muttered an expletive, heard her mother's sharp gasp.

She was going to kill Pete! How dare he exploit her to sell newspapers!

Immediately she thought of Kharun.

"How bad is it?" she asked.

"Your father's getting a copy of the article faxed through. We'll know more then. He was furious. It was bad enough for his friend to call to make sure you were all right. You need to get this cleared up. Can you call Paul Michaels yourself and tell him it's a mix-up? I've got his phone number right here. Needless to say, your father isn't happy about this."

"Neither am I!"

And she knew for absolute sureness Kharun would be furious.

Especially if it ever got back to the ministers who were so opposed to the oil leases.

Fortunately the tabloid is only a U.S. paper.

"His phone number—"

"Wait, I need to find paper and a pencil." She opened the top drawer of the desk. Neat and tidy, nothing like her own desk at work.

A workplace she would never see again unless it was to wring Pete's neck.

She picked up a pen. There was no paper.

She closed it and opened the top right drawer.

"Looking for something?" The cold voice at the door stopped her instantly.

She looked up into Kharun's glittering eyes. He was angry. Any idiot could see that.

"I'll call you back," she told her mother and hung up the phone.

"Why call back? Why not find what you're looking for while he waits?"

"He? That was my mother."

His patent look of disbelief riled her.

"It was! Call her back yourself if you don't believe me. She wanted to give me a phone number. I was looking for something to write on."

"Try this," he said, tossing the faxed copies of the newspaper article onto the desk.

Sara swallowed hard as she recognized the headline banner. Oh, God, he knew!

Knew and was furious.

She licked her lips nervously. "How did you get a copy?"

He tilted his head slightly. "From Garah Sonharh."

Slowly Sara drew the papers closer. She groaned when she saw the photos and captions. But anger grew as she read the inflammatory article. No wonder Kharun was so furious.

"I didn't write this," she said, standing. "You don't believe I did, do you?"

"Wrote it, collaborated, dictated—it makes no difference. No one but you could have provided all the information—where the villa is, when we would ride, the hurried wedding, tension between family members. No one but you."

"I didn't do it. Pete did."

"He conjured it up out of thin air?"

She hesitated, but she couldn't let Kharun think she'd betray him. "I talked to him once. But only once. He kept calling—"

"What are you doing in this office?" he interrupted, obviously not interested in her explanation.

"Aminna said I could take the call here. It was my mother. She was giving me a phone number to call, and I needed something to write it down on." She drew a deep breath. "I'm not spying on you if that's what you think."

"I'm not sure what I think right now."

"Fine, let me know when you decide." Head held high, she stormed out of the room, going wide around Kharun as if suspecting he'd try to stop her.

But he said nothing. Made no move.

She didn't know whether to be angry at him or not.

She knew she was furious with Pete.

She walked back out onto the patio. Her coffee was lukewarm. The pool mocked her with its memories of another time.

She spun around and headed for her room. Snatching up her purse, she left. She'd go see her parents and sort this out.

And she'd call Pete Steede from the privacy of her parents' suite.

Hesitating only a second as she left the villa, she wished Kharun believed her. Wished he'd stood by her.

But why should he? She'd messed this up like she did everything.

Yet it was a thousand times worse this time. She loved him. She would do nothing to cause him harm.

But would he ever come to see her as anyone but the aggravating woman who'd thrown a wrench into the workings of his negotiations?

And how would that blasted article affect his relationship with his uncle's ministers? Or his uncle himself?

She looked at the villa. Would she ever come back?

Highly unlikely.

Kharun's car was parked in front, his chauffeur seated in the driver's seat, reading.

She opened the back door and ignored his start of surprise.

"Presentation Hotel," she said, settling in as if she had every right to do so. She prayed he'd comply and not verify her destination with Kharun. The sooner she was away the better.

He nodded, tossed aside the newspaper and started the car.

In moments, she was on her way. It was hard not to look back. Harder still to keep the tears at bay. Maybe it was better this way. Better to leave him, try to clear up the mess Steede had caused and then stay with her parents until the leases were signed, sealed and delivered.

"What the hell do you mean she's gone?" Kharun roared. Aminna stood in the doorway, her face impassive despite his anger.

"Sargon drove her to the Presentation Hotel."

"He didn't check with me first?"

"Why should he? She's your wife. She needed a ride. He's returned and is waiting to take you back to your office when you're ready."

Kharun ran his fingers through his hair and tried to think. His thought processes were short-circuited—thanks to Sara Kinsale bak Rijad. Like they'd been almost since he met her. Now this.

Conclusive evidence she'd betrayed him? Or a woman prudently staying out of range until his anger cooled?

Think!

For all he knew she and her mother had been making lunch plans on the phone.

If she'd been speaking with her mother.

He hated not knowing what to believe.

The phone rang again. He'd been fielding calls ever since Garah left his office—no doubt to spread the word about the tabloid pictures. Kharun'd already placated his uncle, and Hamin. And his aunt. At least he thought he'd placated his aunt. Time would tell.

In the meantime, he needed to see Sara.

He nodded to Aminna and paced to the window, trying to think. In retrospect, maybe he should have followed Piers's advice way back at the beginning. Shipped her off somewhere and not told a soul.

An idea glimmered. Slowly Kharun relaxed. He'd give Sara until tonight. If she didn't return, then he'd go to get her.

"I don't understand, Sara."

"Mom, trust me on this, okay?"

"But you didn't bring a suitcase or anything. How can you plan to stay the night? What would Kharun say?"

"He'll be glad to have me out of his hair."

"Why? Ever since you got here this morning, you've done little more than make two phone calls and pace around on the carpet so much I think it's wearing thin. You didn't eat enough dinner to keep a bird alive."

"The carpet's fine."

"But you're not."

Sara looked at her mother and almost gave way to tears. But she kept them in. She'd made the mess she was in, and it was up to her to get herself out. She couldn't keep running to Mommy.

"I'm fine."

Roberta shook her head. "I know, you don't want to talk about it. Fine. But I'm here if you need me. And so's your father."

"Thanks." Sara smiled as best she could and paced

to the window.

Her father hadn't been at dinner, finishing up some things, he'd told his wife. At least she'd been spared having to talk to him about the stupid tabloid situation.

Her conversation with Pete had been less than satisfactory. There was no changing the newspaper once it hit the stands. Now there was only damage control. And a promise to sue him to kingdom come if he didn't print a retraction.

Not that it would do much good. Retractions were never front-page headlines.

Her father entered the suite. "Hello, Sara, I didn't know you were here. But you can hear the news when I tell your mother."

Roberta greeted her husband. "What news?"

"The leases were approved this afternoon. We lost a few concessions thanks to Kharun's tough negotiations, but we now have the exclusive rights for the next ten years. Work will start before the end of the month."

"Darling, that's wonderful! Does that mean we can go home soon?"

"As soon as next week."

Sara felt as if she'd been struck.

It was over. There was no reason to continue their marriage.

There'd be no reason for Kharun to seek her out tonight or wonder where she was. He was probably congratulating himself that he didn't even have to tell her to go, that she'd left on her own.

"That's great, Dad," she said brightly. Her face was going to crack if she didn't get away from her parents.

She could only fake a smile for so long.

"I'm tired. I think I'll go to bed. Good night."

"What's going on?" Samuel asked as she fled the room.

"I'm not sure," her mother replied as Sara shut the door to the room she'd used her first night in Kamtansin.

Leaning against the cool wood, Sara let the tears well into her eyes, hoping the pain in her heart would ease enough to let her find oblivion in sleep.

She'd held heaven in her hands—and lost it.

"Oh, Kharun," she whispered.

He hadn't called, had made no effort to even find her, much less ask her to return home.

Now that the leases were approved, there was no reason to see him again.

Oh how she wanted to. How fervently she wished she could be with him forever.

And she wished she could explain, make sure he knew she hadn't betrayed him. That she'd lived up to her commitment.

A knock sounded on the door to the hallway. She pushed away from the door connecting to the sitting room of the suite and crossed the spacious bedroom. Was it the maid to turn down the bed?

She opened the door, shocked to see two uniformed men standing there.

"Sara Kinsale?" one asked.

"Yes."

"Please come with us."

"Who are you? Where do you want me to go?"

"Please come with us."

The second man reached out to take her arm in a firm grasp, pulling her from the room. His actions reminded her of the prison guard.

"Wait!" She pulled against his hand, but he was too strong. She had to tell her parents. She couldn't disappear. Not again.

The door closed behind them and they half carried, half dragged her down the hall. For a moment, she wondered if she was being returned to jail.

Had Kharun reneged on his promise to her because he thought she'd betrayed him with Pete?

"I can't go with you," she said, trying to pull free.

His grip was too solid.

When they bypassed the regular elevators and took the freight elevator, she got scared. Her parents didn't know she wasn't in her room. It would be morning before they discovered her gone. Where would she be?

Before she knew it, she was thrust between the two men in a fast-moving car. It headed away from the city and into the desert.

Sara's thoughts swirled. She had to get away, get to a phone.

Call the American embassy? she thought hysterically. How many times had she asked to do that before?

Where were they going? And why?

The city lights soon behind them, only the slash of the headlights of the car cut through the darkness.

Sara gave up demanding to know what was happening. She suspected only the one man knew any English and that had only been at a very basic level.

Despite her worry, her fear, she was exhausted. The turmoil of the tabloid fiasco, trying to placate her mother, fear of what these men planned, the monotony of riding through the darkness wore her down. Slowly her eyes closed.

Before she fell asleep, however, the car slowed.

Snapping her eyes open, she stared around her. She could see nothing in the dark. The star-studded sky ended in the far horizon dissolving into inky blackness. No lights shone, no buildings were silhouetted against the night sky.

The car stopped, and the driver said something in Arabic. The man to her right opened his door and stepped out, motioning for Sara.

She slowly scooted across the seat and stood. The air was warm, a light breeze blew—but the scent of the sea was missing. This was dry, clear air.

"Why did we stop?"

"We wait," he said.

"For what?"

He shrugged, reached for a cigarette and lit it.

Sara leaned against the car, wondering if she dare try to make a run. She had no idea where she was, or how far from Staboul they were. But the faint glow back from where they came showed her where the city was. On foot it might not take her longer than four or five days' walking.

Her shoes weren't up to it though her long pants would keep sunburn at bay.

She was getting goofy, she thought. She would have no chance to walk back to Staboul—she had no water.

And she doubted the men who abducted her would stand idly by while she tried to run away.

She heard a drumming sound and looked around, trying to figure out what it was and from where it was coming.

A horse. What was a horse doing out here in the middle of nowhere?

It was coming closer. The man put out his cigarette and said something to the man in the car. The engine started again.

Sara turned to get back into the vehicle, but he stopped her.

"No, you wait." He climbed inside and closed the door. The driver turned on his headlights.

Turning to face the sound, Sara waited, resigned, wondering what would happen next.

Eighteen

In only a moment she saw the horse and rider outlined against the stars. The horse looked huge. The rider was dressed in traditional Arab garb, complete with a folded scarf across his face. Only his eyes were visible in the glow of the headlights.

She reached for the door handle. She didn't want to be left at the mercy of some desert raider. Was she to be spirited away, never to be heard from again?

The car was locked. Once the men saw the rider, the car pulled away.

Sara felt as if her last hope was disappearing.

The horse took a step forward, then another. The rider said nothing. Sara's heart beat rapidly. Glancing on either side, she saw no shelter, no place to hide.

"Come." The man reached out a hand.

Sara took a step back. "I don't think so."

"No adventure?"

She stopped, stared. "Kharun?"

"Come."

She couldn't believe her ears. Was it him? But what would he be doing out in the middle of nowhere? She tried to see if the horse was Satin Magic, but it was too dark.

"Come."

The hint of impatience convinced her. She'd recognize that tone anywhere.

She reached up and in seconds sat sideways in front of him. She was barely in place before he drew her close and turned the horse around. Then they were flying across the desert.

She hoped he knew where they were going in the inky darkness.

Not that it mattered. It was exhilarating, riding along the vast empty space, the wind in her face, the stars like distant diamonds overhead, Kharun's arms tightly around her. She closed her eyes, savoring every moment, committing everything to memory. This was an experience she never wanted to forget.

Sara wasn't certain how long they rode, but when he slowed, she looked around. No sounds met her ears, except the jingle of the horse's bridle. No building rose.

"Where are we?" she asked.

Kharun pulled the horse to a stop and eased her to the ground, dismounting to stand beside her a second later.

"A place where no one else will find us," he said.

She looked at him. "No one?" She almost squeaked it out.

"You said you wanted to see the desert, I've brought you." Swiftly he unsaddled the horse and tethered him.

He took her arm gently in one hand and led her around a low mound.

"Wait here a minute." He lifted the flap to the large

tent and entered. In only seconds, a warm glow emanated.

Sara lifted the flap and followed without waiting for Kharun.

The inside stunned her. Rich Persian carpets covered the ground. Tapestries hung from the back wall, their vibrant colors reflecting the lamplight. A large bed was on one side, draped in gauzy netting. The center brass table gleamed in the light, fruits and nuts heaped in bowls.

"Wow." She lifted her gaze to Kharun.

He stood like a bold desert raider in the midst of the splendor. His robes swirled around him as he turned and stared at her, his hands on his hips. He removed the covering from his face, but the rest was pure Arabian fantasy.

Her heart skipped into high gear. Her blood raced through her veins faster than ever. She was almost light-headed.

He'd been angry when last she'd seen him.

He didn't look angry now.

Involuntarily her gaze moved to the bed.

"All the comforts of home," she said. She'd meant to be sarcastic. Instead the throaty sound of her voice was sultry, enticing, sexy.

Slowly she smiled, hoping he didn't guess how nervous she was.

"Why are we here?" she asked.

"I want some time alone together, only the two of us. The negotiations are concluded."

"I heard. So our marriage is over?"

He tilted his head slightly, then drew the headpiece off and carelessly tossed it to a cushion. His dark hair was mussed. Sara's fingers almost ached with desire to tousle it some more, to touch him, feel his heat and strength.

"So, do you mind telling me what we're doing here?" she asked.

"You haven't seen the desert. I wouldn't want you to go home without experiencing all my country offers."

The delight she'd experienced was being with Kharun.

"Aren't you worried I'll take photos and send them to the newspaper? Or report this abduction as some nefarious deed?"

He laughed, his teeth startling white when compared to his tanned skin. "You said you didn't write that article."

"Nor dictate nor collaborate. You seem to be taking this better now than this morning."

"Perhaps," he said, motioning to one cushion near the brass table. "Care to sit?"

She watched him warily for a moment, then nodded, moving to sink on the soft pillow. It felt awkward to sit that low, but was surprisingly comfortable. She looked at the food on the table, at the lamp, anywhere but at Kharun.

He sat beside her, crowding her. He could have sat opposite.

"How did you do all this?" she asked, sweeping her arm to indicate the tent and the decorations.

"I keep the tent for a retreat. It's kept clean and

stocked for me. Food's kept for Satin Magic, as well. When I want to use it, I let the caretaker know, and he disappears until I leave."

"So we really are alone in the middle of the desert?"

"We really are all alone. Does that concern you?"

He leaned closer. Sara could feel the heat from his body envelope her. His breath caressed her cheeks as she looked up into his dark eyes. Her own breath caught.

"No." It came out almost a whisper.

"Good." He closed the distance between them and kissed her.

His touch was all she'd ever dreamed of, inflaming her senses, building desire and passion to blend with the love she already felt growing and encompassing her entire being.

She returned his kiss, meeting him halfway, reveling in the sensations that threatened to catapult her into a realm of hedonistic pleasure only recently known before.

His hand brushed back her hair as he held her face for the kisses that rained down on her. Then he forged a trail of fire and ice as he kissed and nibbled down her neck, to focus on the rapid pulse point at the base of her throat that seemed to fascinate him.

Maybe she wasn't the only one in this fantasy.

She should do something practical about returning to the capital and arranging her trip home.

But Sara didn't feel the least bit practical. She craved his touch like she would crave water in the desert. Maybe because he was as important to her life.

"Tonight is ours," he said.

"Yes." She would agree to anything he said, as long

as he kept kissing her.

He rose and lifted her in his arms to push through the netting and lay her on the bed.

It was incredibly soft—and large. More room than the two of them needed, she thought hazily as he joined her. When he kissed her again, Sara stopped thinking. She had one last night. She was going to enjoy every second of being with Kharun.

Dawn was breaking in the east when Kharun woke Sara with a gentle kiss.

"Um?" She burrowed closer. She didn't want to wake up. Didn't want to face the day.

"Come and see the dawn. There's nothing like it as it spreads over the desert, the light faint at first, then growing bolder. The temperature's cool—nothing like the searing heat of midday. And the shadows allow your imagination to fly."

Her imagination was flying right now, and it centered on the two of them in bed, not getting up, going into the cold dawn air.

She didn't want her last night with Kharun to end. She wanted time to stand still.

"Go away," she said grumpily. If he didn't want to stretch it out, so be it. But she could.

"Come on, you'll love it."

"I love you," she mumbled.

Then froze, instantly awake, though she kept her eyes shut. Tightly shut. Oh, she hadn't really said that out loud, had she?

She held her breath. Please, please, please, she thought, don't let me have said that out loud.

His finger tilted her face up. She kept her eyes shut. "Sara?"

With a sigh, she slowly opened her eyes. His dark eyes stared down into hers, his expression unreadable.

"Well now that I'm awake, I might as well get up and see that sunrise. Then we can go back to Staboul and I can make arrangements to head for home," she grumbled, starting to get out of bed.

Their legs were tangled and Kharun clamped a hand on her arm. She couldn't move.

"Maybe we need to talk," he suggested.

"Maybe we need to get on with our lives," she replied. "Let me up or the sun will beat us."

"We have a few minutes. You know we signed the oil leases yesterday."

She nodded, longing to escape, longing to leave before she made an even bigger fool of herself. He had to have heard, yet he said nothing. His way of letting her down easy?

"Yes. So I can go home today."

"I brought Alia with Satin Magic. I thought we could stay here for a few days. We have food, water, and the desert to ourselves."

She blinked. "Stay here? Are you nuts? There's no reason to stay here. I should make airline reservations. My parents will fly home soon and I'll go with them. I have a job to get back to—" Not after she'd burned her bridges.

"I thought you were working with Tamil on the tourist project here. That's your job."

She pushed up on one elbow and stared at him.

"What's going on?"

"I'd thought you'd stay."

"Why?"

"You love me."

She flopped back on the pillow and closed her eyes again. He had heard!

"And you have a job to do," he said.

"I didn't tell Pete about us. He tweaked some of the stuff I told him and blew it out of proportion."

"Once I cooled down, and Jasmine yelled at me, I suspected that." There was definitely the sound of amusement in his tone.

She opened her eyes and glared at him.

"Are you laughing at me?"

He shook his head, but the laughter lurked in his eyes.

"Kharun, what's going on? Is this marriage over or not?"

"Ah, that's what I wanted to talk about. Don't you think people would find it odd to end it the day after the negotiations were concluded?"

"As compared to when?"

"I don't know, sometime later, so people won't think it was a false marriage."

"Sometime later?" she asked suspiciously.

"Yes."

"How much later?"

"I don't know." He looked at her sharply. "Fifty or sixty years."

She stared at him, her heart racing. Had she heard him correctly? She cleared her throat.

"That's sort of a long time."

"I'm game if you are." He brushed his fingers through her hair, smiling that sexy smile that turned her bones to mush. "I love you, too, Sara. I fought it at first. One day I'll tell you about a woman I thought I loved before. But she doesn't belong with us today. I want you to stay with me forever, but I'll settle for fifty years with an option to renegotiate."

"And you are so good at negotiating," she murmured, moving to meet him halfway with a kiss that sealed their future. "I love you, Kharun."

"I was hoping you did." His kiss made her blood sing and her heart blossomed with happiness and love.

Then he ended the kiss. "Time's up. Come and see the sunrise," he said seconds later, throwing back the covers.

It was cold. She frowned and tried to pull the covers back, but he lifted her out of bed and placed her on her feet.

"Hurry."

"I'd rather stay in bed."

"We'll come back." He tossed her his shirt, the loose one from the night before. Sara slipped it on, tied it closed at the neck and pushed the sleeves up so her hands showed.

"Nothing's been decided. We have to discuss this," she said.

"We'll have the rest of our lives to discuss anything you wish. But right now, come and see the sunrise. Later this morning—before it gets too hot, we'll go riding."

He pulled on his pants and waited impatiently by the

door. Staring at his chest, she remembered last night. Happiness and love blossomed inside, spilling out in her delightful grin.

Kharun loved her! Miracles still happened.

"I thought you were furious with me," she said walking toward him.

"I was. But love's stronger than anger. And once I looked at things rationally and remembered everything you'd ever said I knew you'd never have betrayed me."

He'd had faith in her even when the evidence pointed the other way.

She'd never had that before. It was amazing how wonderful it felt.

For the first time in a long while, Sara didn't feel like a flake.

"Thank you."

"For?"

"Believing in me."

"And loving you?"

She laughed in joy. "That, too. That most of all." She ran across the distance separating them and flung herself into his arms. "I love you so much. I didn't want to leave, but thought it best if I left before you kicked me out."

"Revisionist history? I believe you stormed out, I certainly didn't kick you out."

"Well, I thought you would have, after seeing that damaging article."

"It'd never have happened. I knew long ago you were the one I wanted. I told you, one cannot fight destiny. I wasn't sure you felt the same way—especially after our hasty marriage."

"What are you talking about? You thought I was a spy!"

He laughed softly. "Never that. You don't have the skills to be a spy."

"I resent that!"

"With that honey hair and your flair, you could never fade into the background like a good spy needs to."

"Well, you didn't trust me."

"At first, maybe, but neither did you trust me," he countered.

She was quiet for a moment, mulling over what he'd said, afraid to let herself believe they'd stay married the rest of their lives. Could he truly mean it?

"You forced me into an arranged marriage," she said.

"I hear they can be the best kind. Ours will be the best."

"I love you," she whispered.

"I love you," he replied promptly.

He kissed her, then took her hand to lead her outside. "Forget your uncertainties. I'll do all in my power to see we have a wonderful life together. Promise me you'll stay."

She smiled, her joy reflected in her eyes. "I promise!"

Sara stepped forward to greet the dawn, not only of a new day, but of her new life.

A life of love and happiness with Kharun, her own desert sheikh.

More Books by Barbara McMahon

Cowboy Hero
Cowboy Hero Series
The Cowboy Next Door
Cowboy's Bride
One Stubborn Cowboy
Crazy About a Cowboy
Never Doubt a Cowboy
Cowboy Marshal
Summer Cowboy
Second Chance Cowboy
Movie Star Cowboy

Cowboy Heroes Boxed Set Books 1-3
Cowboy Heroes Boxed Set Books 4-6
Cowboy Heroes Boxed Set Books 7-9

The Harts of Texas Series
Rebel Heart
Tangled Hearts
Reckless Heart

Harts of Texas Box Set: Books 1-3

Ultimate Billionaires Series
The Cynical Sheikh
Falling for the Sheikh
A Sheikh of Her Own
The Unforgettable Sheikh

Ultimate Billionaires Box Set Books 1-2
Ultimate Billionaires Box Set Books 3-4
Ultimate Billionaires Box Set Books 1-4

Rocky Point Series
Rocky Point Legacy
Rocky Point Reunion
Rocky Point Promise
Rocky Point Hero

Rocky Point Inn
Rocky Point Dawn

Rocky Point Boxed Set Books 1-3
Rocky Point Boxed Set Books 4-6

The Talmadge Sisters Series
Letters to Caroline
Michelle's Marriage Deal
Trusting Abby

Tropical Escapes Series
Island Rendezvous
Come into the Sun
Island Paradise

Destination Romance Boxed Set

Sweet Romance Stand-alone Collection
Because of You
Cowboy Charade
I'll Take Forever
Jared's Promise
Mail Order Bride
Not Really Married
Sweet Meant To Be
The Cowboy Comes Home
The Paper Marriage
Trusting Jake
The Banished Bride

A Sweet Clean Christmas Romance Collection
The Christmas Cop
The Cowboy's Special Christmas
A Soldier's Christmas
A Teaspoon of Mistletoe
The Christmas Locket
A Key West Christmas (*coming soon*)

Love And All The Trimmings